STRAITJACKET MEMORIES

MICHAEL WEST

Hydra
Publications

For Jerry, Maurice, Natalie, Nikki, Rodney, and most of all Sara.
Thank you all for sharing in my insanity.

"For the most wild, yet most homely narrative which I am about to pen, I neither expect nor solicit belief. Mad indeed would I be to expect it, in a case where my very senses reject their own evidence. Yet, mad am I not — and very surely do I not dream. But tomorrow I die, and today I would unburthen my soul. My immediate purpose is to place before the world, plainly, succinctly, and without comment, a series of mere household events. In their consequences, these events have terrified — have tortured — have destroyed me. Yet I will not attempt to expound them. To me, they have presented little but Horror — to many they will seem less terrible than barroques. Hereafter, perhaps, some intellect may be found which will reduce my phantasm to the commonplace — some intellect more calm, more logical, and far less excitable than my own, which will perceive, in the circumstances I detail with awe, nothing more than an ordinary succession of very natural causes and effects." ~Edgar Allan Poe

ALSO BY MICHAEL WEST

Harmony, Indiana Novels

The Wide Game

Cinema of Shadows

Spook House

Legacy of the Gods Novels

Poseidon's Children

Hades' Disciples

Zeus' Warriors

Kronos' Return

Short Story Collections

Skull Full of Kisses

Straitjacket Memories

INTRODUCTION

When you opened this book*, I hope the spine creaked, much like that famous door from *The Inner Sanctum*. During the radio show's eleven-year run (1941 to 1952), guest voices included the likes of Boris Karloff, Peter Lorre, and the great Orson Welles, but it was that door—with its rusty, unoiled hinges—that became the real star. Whenever you heard its terrible, ear-splitting creak, you knew you were in for a tale! Some were creepy, some were weird, others interesting, and still more were downright terrifying. I hope, faithful readers, you will have a similar experience with this collection you hold now in your hands.

There are ten more tales gathered here for you to enjoy. All were written after the release of my first book of short fiction, *Skull Full of Kisses*. That collection really opened doors for me, and first and foremost, I have to thank Dale Murphy of Graveside Tales, the original publisher, for taking a chance on an unknown. All the success I have enjoyed in recent years has been due, in some fashion, to that book and how well it was received by both critics and readers alike.

Since the publication of that collection, I have had requests from various editors for all sorts of tales, invitations to one anthology after another, each project more fascinating than the last. I owe all of those editors my undying gratitude. I could name them all for you here, but I won't bore you with that very long list. Suffice it to say that each of them saw something in my writing, and they believed that I had great stories to tell, even when I wasn't so sure myself.

OK...so that's enough of that noise. You're not here to hear about me and my career, or to read something that comes off like an awards show acceptance speech. No. You, my faithful readers, are here for a good story. Several, I hope. So let's get on with it, shall we?

The door is now open, and you are in for a few wild tales! Some are creepy. Some are weird. Some you might find interesting, and still others, downright terrifying. All the old familiar archetypes are here: ghosts and witches, monsters and shapeshifters, vampires, mummies, and zombies too, but none are exactly what you'd expect. So please, feel free to step inside and have a look around. Yes, it's dark in here, I know, but if you stay on the path, I'm sure you'll be fine. At least, I think you will be...

Michael West

Indianapolis, Indiana
June, 2014

*If you are holding an eReader instead of an actual book, you didn't get to hear that wonderful creaking sound when you broke the spine, but I hope you will enjoy these tales all the same.

ISBN Number: 978-1-948374-84-2

Hydra Publications
Goshen, Kentucky 40026
www.hydrapublications.com

Publisher's Note:
Straitjacket Memories is a work of fiction. All names, characters, and places are
the product of the author's imagination, used in a fictitious manner. Any
resemblances to actual persons, places, locales, events, etc. are purely
coincidental.

DON'T LET THE BED BUGS BITE

"My wife's been missing for two weeks now," the new patient said as he slid all the cushions off Dr. Helen Burr's couch and onto the office floor. The patient's name was Kozak. Anthony Kozak. Helen didn't need to look at his file to know that. His name and face were all over the news. "The police are looking for her, but they won't find her, and God help me, I don't *want* them to find her."

Helen said nothing; she sat in her chair, scrutinizing his actions.

Kozak took a small flashlight from his pocket and explored the upholstery, illuminating every dark nook and cranny. Satisfied, he returned light to pocket, cushions to couch, and took a seat. He refused to lean back, however, refused to relax in any way.

The picture on television showed a handsome man, rugged, with faded blue eyes. The face Helen now studied was tight, gaunt. And those pale eyes now swam the bottom of deep, dark wells; they searched the room like a frightened animal's, and when they found the office door, they never left it, as if Kozak were waiting for someone to enter, or wanted to keep his only escape route in sight.

After a few moments, Helen broke the silence. "Why is that?"

Kozak blinked and those sunken eyes locked with hers. "Excuse me?"

"Why don't you want them to find her?"

"Because she's not my wife anymore...she's not the woman I loved."

Past tense. Helen didn't frown, didn't show any suspicion what-so-ever. Like a surgeon, she too wore a mask, a professional face that conveyed expertise, conveyed sympathy and understanding. Only by gaining the patient's trust could she ever hope to find the truth.

"The police think that I've...that I've done something to her. I can't say I blame them. After all, a woman goes missing in the middle of the night...without taking her purse, her driver's license, her credit cards and cell phone...and the first thing they're going to do is suspect foul play, to point a finger at the husband and label him some kind of monster. But I'm not the monster here, Doc. I didn't kill my wife. She's out there somewhere, oh yes, she's just not the woman I married."

Oh, I'm sure she's out there. Buried in some shallow grave, no doubt. The question is 'why?' Helen cleared her throat and glanced at Kozak's file. "You've never seen a psychiatrist before?"

"No. I've never had the need."

"And do you prefer to be called Anthony, or Tony?"

"Tony."

She nodded, closed the file, and gave him her full attention. "Could you tell me what *did* happen to your wife, Tony?"

He hesitated, then said, "That's why I came here, Doc, to tell you what happened, to tell you the *truth*."

"That's good, Tony, because there are no secrets in my office. I want you to tell me everything. It's the only way I can help you."

"I don't think anyone can help me, Doc." His eyes drifted back to the door. "But I need to tell someone, before I really do go crazy."

"I'm here to listen," Helen assured him, putting on a smile. She motioned to the cushions, congratulated herself on having waited so long to bring it up. "But first, I am curious...why did you take my couch apart before you sat down? What were you looking for?"

"Bed bugs," he whispered.

Helen's professional facade slipped a bit at that. She'd expected him to say bugs all right, but she thought it would be of the FBI or UFO variety. *Been hanging around paranoid schizo-phrenics far too long, dear*. "Do you always check for bed bugs before sitting down on strange furniture?"

He chuckled bitterly. "You know, when I was a child, I didn't even know that bed bugs were a real thing. I thought they were some kind of fairy tale, you know? When my mother tucked me in at night, she'd say,'Goodnight, sleep tight, don't let the bed bugs bite.'"

Helen nodded, preserving the masquerade. "My mother told me the same thing."

"But they *are* real, Doc. And now...now they're everywhere. Hotels. College dorms. Movie theaters. Even clothing stores. They come out of the dark, latch themselves on, and they...they feed on your blood." His face curdled. "Disgusting."

Helen glanced at the timer on the coffee table between them. "You were going to tell me about your wife?"

Kozak smiled. "Her name was Rosanna, like that 80's song. I called her Rose. My perfect Rose."

He wiped at his eyes with the back of his hand and Helen offered him a box of Kleenex.

"Thank you." Kozak blew his nose, cleared his throat, and continued. "Anyway, we loved to travel the world together, we did everything together, my Rose and I...coral reefs in the Caribbean, the Olympics in Greece, Valentine's Day on the Eiffel Tower. And this year, for our anniversary, we went on safari in Africa."

Helen offered a smile. "Sounds incredible."

"Oh, it was. *She* was." His face filled with genuine light, but it soon clouded over again. "She picked up the bed bug in Africa.

"We were always so careful too. First thing I'd do when we checked into a hotel was pull back the bedding and take a look at the mattress, this was before we even brought our luggage into the room. And even after I'd checked things out, we'd *never* put a suitcase on the bed. Rose even went so far as to put all of our clothes in big Zip-lock bags just to be sure. She didn't want bugs of any kind to get in, especially not those little vampires."

He chuckled, then wiped at his eyes again. "That's what Rose always called them: 'little vampires.'"

"A pretty accurate description," Helen agreed.

"Yeah, well, Rose always had a way of summing things up." Kozak's eyes crept back to the office door. "Anyway, the vacation started off well. She saw her first wild elephant and giraffe...she loved all animals, but especially giraffes. She had that picture of the mother kissing the baby giraffe on the head." He smiled again, but it was gone in a wink. "That first night in the hotel, I did everything the same...checked the bedding and the headboard...and there were no bugs and none of those brown spots they shit out. Everything looked clean. The bed even had mosquito netting, just in case any of those bloodsuckers got in the room."

"Mosquitoes would be a larger concern in Africa," Helen told him. "They carry malaria. Bed bugs, while unpleasant, don't spread disease."

"This was no ordinary bed bug."

"I see."

"No, you don't." Pain and fear burned in the windows of his eyes, like a housefire in the middle of the night. "And I didn't either. At least, not at first."

"When *did* you notice something was wrong?"

"The next morning." Kozak swallowed, wrung his hands, then went on, "I slept through the night, practically comatose. You ever hear that old saying, 'The night the kudzu takes your farm, you sleep like the dead?'"

Helen nodded. She studied each gesture and mannerism, trying to decode non-verbal clues as he spoke.

"Well, when we finally woke up, Rose had these red bumps...*bites*...they were on her neck and her...her breast. And drops of blood dotted the white sheet on her side of the bed."

"And you?" Helen asked.

"Huh?"

"You were bitten as well?"

"No. It didn't touch me."

"Don't you find that odd?" Helen asked gently, trying her best not to be confrontational. "If you were in the same bed, I would think they—"

"It didn't want me," Kozak told her. "It wanted *her*."

The statement caught Helen by surprise. For an instant, her mask fell away and she gaped at him, sure she'd misunderstood. "The *bed bug* wanted—?"

"I told you, this was no ordinary bed bug."

She looked down at his file, tried to wrestle her professional facade back into place. "Did Rose have some kind of allergic reaction to the bites? Something the local hospital would have documented?"

Kozak waved his hand. "No, no...we didn't go to any hospital. No witch doctors. We just used some antiseptic cream and she was fine. I went to the hotel to complain and they gave us a free night's stay in a new room, the honeymoon suite."

Helen glanced up and pushed the hair from her face. "I'm sure you checked that room out as well?"

"You're damned right I did! I went over every square inch of it and didn't find a thing."

"And did anything unusual happen that night?"

"I was asleep the moment my head it the pillow, just like the night before. Slept like the dead. And the next morning, Rose had fresh bites. I couldn't figure out how she could sleep through it, you know? I mean, something's crawling on you, eating you alive, and you don't even notice?"

"It can happen."

"Honestly?"

"Certainly. People have slept through all sorts of accidents and natural disasters. Sleeping through a bug bite is no more outlandish. You yourself said you slept like the dead."

"So I did."

Helen gave the digital clock another quick glance. Their time was passing quickly. "What happened next?"

"Next? Next, I went to the hotel staff to give them a piece of my mind! The manager spoke English, and he was all apologies, said they ran a clean establishment and that this kind of thing just didn't happen, but the other staff members were staring at us, whispering things. I didn't speak the language, so I had no idea what they were saying—complaining about the crazy Americans for all I knew—but one word kept coming up again and again: *Adze*."

"And you knew what that word meant?"

"I thought it was just local folklore, but after what happened, after what I saw—"

"You thought *what* was just folklore?"

"The *Adze* is a kind of vampire."

"Their word for bed bugs?"

"No, a *real* vampire, but it can take the form of an insect, a bed bug."

Helen was stunned. She combed her hair with her fingers

again, trying to fix her slipped façade, trying not to let him see. This was no drug abusing actor, no socialite trying to replace Daddy's love with a spree on Rodeo Drive, nor any of the other high profile clients she'd made her name with. No. This, this was the mother lode! This was a case on which she could write a bestseller. This was a case that could make her career. She opened her mouth to speak, then stopped herself, needing to find the right path to take before proceeding.

Kozak went on without her, "We took the next flight home, and, again, I did everything I was supposed to. We kept the suitcases in the garage and all of our clothes went straight into the laundry, even the stuff we didn't wear. They say it only takes a good thirty minutes of hot water and the dryer to kill those fuckers, and I wasn't taking any chances. No bugs were getting into *our* house. Anything that we couldn't wash, all Rose's delicates, I put in the freezer. They say a week in the freezer will kill them just as good as thirty minutes in the dryer. Well, that's what they say.

"Anyway, Rose was very tired. We both were. The whole day had been a blur of long flights and airport layovers, and the jet lag really hit us, so she went to bed, and, after dealing with the luggage, I joined her. It was so good to be back in my own bed, Doc."

"I know that feeling," Helen agreed, flashing her understanding grin, watching his sunken eyes. "And you slept well?"

"No. I had a horrible dream, like something out of the Hammer horror films I saw as a kid."

"Tell me."

Kozak licked his lips. "I dreamed there was someone else in the bedroom with us."

"Someone else? A man or a woman?"

"A man—at least, I think it was a man. He drifted out of the shadows toward the bed, almost as if he were floating"

"Had you seen him before?"

"No. Never."

"Can you describe him to me?"

Kozak shook his head. "It was too dark."

"Well, then how do you know it wasn't someone you'd seen before?"

"The eyes, Doc. They glowed red in the darkness, like the eyes of an animal caught in headlights. They looked—they looked *hungry*. He went to Rose's side of the bed and he—he just stood there, *watching* her."

"Did he say anything?"

"No. Nothing."

"Did you say anything to him?"

"No. I couldn't talk, couldn't move, I couldn't even breath. All I could do was watch as he reached out and groped Rose's breast. His fingers were long—too long—and the nails were hooked, like bird claws. And when he bent down, I could hear him sink his teeth into her."

"And what did Rose do?"

"At first, I thought she was still asleep, but then she made these sounds—heavy breathing, and then moaning, like she was enjoying it, like it was *sex*."

"And you were unable to stop him," Helen said. "All you could do was lay there—impotent."

Kozak glared at her. "What's that supposed to mean?"

Helen chose her next words with care, spoke in a gentle tone, "Just that you were powerless to help the woman you loved."

"Yeah, well, I tried to scream at him to leave her alone, but like I said, there was no sound. And then the dark form started moving and twitching all over, and I realized that it wasn't a man at all anymore...it was a crawling mound of bugs—hundreds, maybe thousands of them. The shadow lost its shape, melted as the bugs spread out to cover Rose, as they crawled toward *me*. I tried to sit up, to get away, and when I did, I found myself awake. The room was empty except for me and—and Rose."

"Was Rose awake too?"

"No. She was laying there with her back to me, and I thought I saw something move."

"In the bed?"

"No, in *Rose*. I knew it was the bed bugs. They were crawling back and forth across her spine, moving just beneath her skin, like they hadn't just bitten her but—but had actually burrowed their way into her flesh." Kozak shuddered and scratched his forearm as if it itched. "I reached over to turn on the light, and when I looked back, they were gone. So I searched for new bites and I didn't find any. In fact, the old bites were almost healed."

"Because it was a dream," Helen offered.

He smiled at that, but there was no joy in it. "All in my head, right Doc?"

"Images from your unconscious mind, yes. Images culled from your African experience: the bed bug bites, the superstitious talk of vampires—"

His eyes drifted back to the door. "That's what I thought too...at first."

"But you don't think that way now?"

He went on as if he hadn't heard the question, "I brought Rose breakfast in bed, but she didn't touch it. She slept most of the day away. And when I went back up to check on her in the late afternoon, she was so pale. I felt her forehead to see if she was feverish, but she was *cold*—cold and clammy. I thought she had some kind of virus, that the bed bugs had given her some disease."

"Did you have a doctor look at her this time? Did they run any medical tests?"

"I carried her down to the car and rushed her to the Emergency room, you bet I did, and after running a bunch of tests, they came back and told me that she was anemic."

Helen paused. If true, the test results would have strengthened Kozak's delusion, making it more difficult to deny. "And how did they treat it? Vitamins? Transfusions? A stay in a hyperbaric chamber?"

"They gave her a transfusion, kept her overnight for observation, then they gave her vitamins to take when she got home."

"Did they say what caused it?"

"They didn't have to. I knew what was going on. The *Adze* had dug in like a tick. It buried itself in her, and she carried it back while it fed on her the whole time. I wanted the doctors to run more tests, to find it if it was still there. And if it wasn't, I wanted them to keep an eye on her so it didn't get to her again. I thought the next time...the next time it would kill her."

A single tear ran down his cheek and he wiped it away with the crumpled Kleenex.

"They wouldn't do it, said they needed the beds and she was well enough to leave. So I took her home, gave her the vitamins, and then I moved a chair over to her side of the bed. I vowed that I would watch over her all night, that I would protect her, but I couldn't stay awake. The woman I love is fighting for her life, and I can't keep my fucking eyes open!"

"Did you have another dream?" Helen asked.

"I wish it was a dream. I wish everything from that moment on was just a nightmare. I wish—I wish I could wake up in my wife's arms and everything could be just like it was before. But this is reality, Doc, and I do know the difference."

Kozak was trembling now.

"I woke up to find the bed empty. I ran through the house screaming her name, 'Rose! *ROSE!*' And when I got to the family room, I saw her standing by the French doors. The doors were open just a crack, and the cold night air made me shiver. She was hunched over, and I could see that she held a cat in her arms. We didn't own any pets, so I thought it was a stray that she found on the back porch. She had a habit of doing that. Letting things in and feeding them."

He chuckled; a hollow, empty sound.

"Anyway, she held this cat up against her face, like she was nuzzling it. I reached over and turned on the light, and then I saw the blood, saw how limp the cat hung in her arms. It was dead. It was some dead thing and she was holding it against her mouth as if she wanted to kiss it goodnight.

"'Rose,' I said, 'What the hell are you doing?'

"Then she lifted her head and the cat's blood slipped down her chin. She'd ripped out its throat. She was drinking from it.

"She looked up at me with these—these glowing red eyes, like the eyes in my dream, but now I knew that it wasn't a dream at all. And when she smiled, I saw how long her teeth had grown—not just the canines like in the vampire movies, but *all* of her teeth!

"She wasn't my wife anymore, Doc. She—she wasn't even *human*."

"What happened next, Tony?"

"I ran. God help me, but I ran right out the door. I got in the car and I drove. I didn't know where I was going and I didn't care, I just kept driving around town until the sun came up, until I thought it was safe to go home. And when I got back, the house was empty. That was two weeks ago."

"When you reported her missing, what did you say to the police?"

"I said I woke up and she was gone. Which is true. At first, I wanted them to find her so that I could cure her. I spent hours on the internet and even went to the local library, going over every volume on African folklore I could find. But once a human is possessed by the *Adze*, there's no hope. No protection. If you capture them in their insect form, you can kill them, but I don't think I could bring myself to do that. Like I said, I've never hurt my wife, Doc, and I never will, but I never want to see that face again as long as I live. Never. Ever."

Helen nodded. Still professional. Still hiding all her theories and suspicions. "How long has it been since you've slept?"

Kozak shrugged. "I don't know."

"You're still scared, aren't you?"

"I've changed all the locks on the doors. I bolt all the windows at night, turn on every light in the house, but I can't shake this feeling that she's going to come back, that she's going to try to make me like her."

The alarm on the coffee table went off, making both of them jump. Helen reached down and fumbled with the buttons until she shut it off.

Kozak wiped at his eyes and stood, clearly happy to be off the couch. "Thank you for listening, Doc. The police keep bringing me in for questioning, and I keep giving them the same old lie. It was good to get it all out, to tell the truth for once."

Helen reached up and touched his arm. "Do you have someone who can stay with you, Tony?"

"No. Rose—she was all I had."

"Then let me prescribe you something," Helen told him. "It will make you less anxious, help you sleep without being so afraid."

He nodded. "Sure. I'd like that. I'd like that a lot."

Helen took out her prescription pad and scribbled the order, thinking as she wrote. She had no proof that he'd done something to his wife, just as there was no way the police could put him in jail. They needed more. "I think we should see each other again in a week, Tony, to see how things are going."

"All right. If you want."

"I do."

Helen handed him the prescription. She watched him fold it, watched him shove it in his wallet, then watched him walk cautiously out the door. She exhaled and smiled; it was genuine, full of excitement. For the next hour, she wrote in Tony Kozak's file. She wrote her theories on spousal abuse, on murder, and how his mind had blamed it on, of all things, African vampires.

A few days later, when a police detective arrived at her office to question her about the session, Helen wasn't really surprised. She put on her professional face and a cooperative smile. "Detective, surely I don't have to remind you that anything Mr. Kozak and I discussed is protected by doctor-client confidentiality."

"And I don't have to tell you, Doctor, that confidentiality doesn't apply if the patient is dead."

The detective took several photographs out of the file tucked under his arm; he put them on Helen's desk for her review.

There was Tony Kozak, lying on his bed, the bed that felt so comfortable upon his return from Africa, the bed that, until two weeks ago, he'd shared with his wife. His eyes were wide, glazed and lifeless. Blood covered his neck and blotted his cheek. There was something clutched in his right hand; one of the close-up photos showed an empty pill bottle that bore Helen's name.

The detective's craggy face regarded her with the same intent interest she'd shown Kozak. "Did he give you any information on the whereabouts of his wife?"

Helen shook her head. "He claimed she was still alive, still out there somewhere. He was afraid of her, in fact. He couldn't sleep at all because of his fear, which is why I wrote him the prescription."

Helen's eyes fixed on Kozak's neck wound; it looked as if his throat had been torn out. She thought of his story, of the cat. "This injury...is it self-inflicted?"

"No. The M.E. confirmed Kozak was already dead from the overdose when that happened."

Helen swiveled in her chair, her gaze skating across the frozen crime scene. *That smudge on his cheek.* She grabbed a magnifying glass to enlarge it. "Is this a lip print?"

"Yes."

Helen stared at the photo, feeling her educated façade coming unhinged, but unable to stop it, unable to believe what she saw. It looked as if someone had kissed Kozak on the cheek, someone wearing far too much red lipstick, but Helen knew it wasn't lipstick.

"That's the vic's blood," the detective told her, "in case you're wondering. And there were traces of saliva in the neck wound. Looks like someone found Kozak dead, then tore his throat out with their teeth before they kissed him goodbye. You think the missing wife is capable of something twisted like that?"

She's going to come back, he said, she's going to try to make me like her.

Helen cleared her throat. "Well, lip print identification is rare, but, as I understand it, it's very similar to fingerprint comparison, and of course, there's DNA in saliva that you can compare with samples of the wife's hair and other items from the home."

The detective nodded. "The lab's working on that as we speak."

"In that case, Detective, I don't see what more I can do to help you."

"You can tell me if Kozak talked about his wife being a magician."

Helen blinked. "Excuse me?"

"All the doors were locked and bolted from the inside, Doctor, including the door to the bedroom. The windows were all latched as well." The detective paged through his notebook, then scratched his forehead. "The only way anyone could've gotten in or out of that place was if they were Houdini."

Helen's blouse grew damp with sweat; it stuck to her back and chest. The magnifying glass trembled in her hand as she went over the photos again and again, studying the tiny gaps between the base of the doors and the blood-stained carpet. When she was finally able to speak, her voice was just a notch above a whisper.

"Or a bug."

FLOWERS IN WINTER

We will *be together.*

The declaration filled Derek's inner ear; a stranger's voice, but he felt its passion as if it were his own. He glanced up Church Street, found red brick silhouetted against gray sky. Shuttered windows peered at him between naked branches. A temporary hospital during the Civil War, the old North house currently served as a historical museum, and though Derek knew exactly how many bricks formed its two-story façade, this was the first time he'd actually laid eyes upon it.

He stood there in the snow, hypnotized, shivering, his desert camouflage making him conspicuous. Beneath his coat, he clutched a bouquet of red roses to his chest, protected their delicate petals from bitter winds. He'd been compelled to buy them, to bring them. He didn't know why, just as he didn't know whose voice echoed through his skull.

I will come to Lewisburg, it promised, and then, over and over again, *I will come for* you.

Soon, the compulsion to enter the house became too strong for Derek to resist. He made his way up the shoveled walkway, lines of wind-blown snow slithering across his path. The front steps were dark and speckled with rock salt.

Inside, warmth enveloped Derek, a lover welcoming him home. The visions that haunted him, however, had been those of an outsider. He stomped his feet on the mat and his eyes darted to and fro, taking in his new surroundings.

In the center of the room, postcards filled wire-framed towers. Off to the left, gas logs blazed in a stone fireplace. Two turn-of-the-century portraits hung above the mantle—a man and a woman. Brass nameplates dubbed them Melville and Claudia Bartlett.

A woman stood behind an antique cash register on the far right—her raven hair pulled back, her pale brow furrowed like drifted snow. She counted boxes of taffy, adjusting her inventory accordingly. "We're closing up for the night," she told him, and barely lifted her head from her bookkeeping. "It's almost four and—"

She froze, held him in a stunned, oblique stare.

Looking into her dark eyes, Derek was struck by a sense of déjà vu, the same feeling he had upon sighting this house for the first time. He glanced down and saw that he held the roses out. He quickly lowered the bouquet, his cheeks warm and red as the petals in his hand.

On the battlefield, he stood his ground in the midst of explosions and sniper fire. But now, in this house, with this intimate stranger, he had a sudden urge to run and forget this madness. He was about to give in when the woman spoke up again, and what she said only added to the mystery.

"After all these years, you've finally come back."

His eyes widened; when he found his voice, it was far too meek for his liking. "You've seen me before?"

"Well, not *you*, no, but..." Her lips blossomed into an odd grin. "Oh, come on. A soldier...*here*...delivering flowers? Did someone put you up to this?"

"I don't know anyone in Lewisburg. I don't even know why I'm here. I just felt this urge to...to..." He stood there a moment, wanting to share, *needing* to share, but he did not care for the skeptical look this woman gave him. He did not care for it at all.

She'll think I'm crazy, trying for a Section 8. Who knows, maybe I am.

"Sorry to have bothered you." Derek marched over to the counter, dropped the roses in front of her, then turned away. "Have a nice evening."

"Now, hold on. Wait a minute."

When he looked back at her, her eyes were downcast, studying his flowers.

"It's not every day a man brings me roses." She brushed the soft petals with her fingers. "You can at least tell me your name."

"Derek. Derek Patterson."

"You really don't know the story, Derek?" She lifted her eyes to him, and it was like something remembered from a dream. "The girl, the soldier...none of it?"

"No."

"If you don't have to run off, I could tell you, give you a quick tour of the house."

"I'd hate to make you go through any trouble, ma'am."

She grinned. "It's Ginny. And it's no trouble."

"Then I think I'd like to hear it," he told her.

I think I need *to hear it.*

Ginny moved out from behind the counter. She wore a black skirt that came down to her ankles and high-heeled boots with silver buckles. "This way."

Derek followed her to a spectacular staircase, admiring the elaborate, hand-carved woodwork. He glanced up at the second floor. It was quite dark. "You mentioned a girl and a soldier?"

"They fell in love," Ginny told him as they mounted the stairs. "Of course, her parents didn't approve. I guess it would be a pretty boring legend if everyone was happy."

She laughed, a shaky giggle that betrayed her nervousness. Was it being alone here with him, Derek wondered, or something else?

"On tours," Ginny resumed, "I like to call the girl Abigail." She took each step slowly, cautiously, the aged wood creaking beneath her feet. "Her parents shipped her off, and she came here to live with her Aunt Claudia and Uncle Melville. They were very strict, especially Melville. He kept Abby locked away. The poor girl, she just laid up there on her bed and cried."

Ginny paused a moment, stared up into the gloom, perhaps realizing that she forgot to turn on the lamps, perhaps not. It almost looked as if she was trying to regain her courage, but that was probably Derek's imagination.

"Then it was Christmas," she said, finally taking the next step, "and they allowed Abby to return home to her parents for the holidays. And wouldn't you know it, her soldier, her true love, was waiting for her."

It was easy for Derek to imagine their tender reunion. How many times had he watched long absent warriors embrace the joyous wives and girlfriends they left behind? Derek could not help but envy them. At the end of the day, he was alone but for the voice of a stranger.

They will never keep us apart.

Ginny clung to the wooden handrail as if it were all that sepa-rated her from the mouth of a very deep well. She went on with her story, her words echoing through the empty foyer. "The soldier—I like to call him John—vowed to follow his love to Lewisburg, promised to take her away from this house, this prison."

They reached the upper level. Outside, the wind howled and the walls groaned against its forceful push; a century-old stale-mate. At either end of the hall, the windows glowed—street-lamps reflecting off the snow, casting bizarre shadows.

Ginny moved to a door on the opposite side of the hallway. She placed her hand on the knob and glanced back at Derek, her eyes sparkling in the dimness. "This was Abby's room."

The door opened with a squeal, short but shrill, and Derek followed Ginny inside. His hands were slick with sweat. He looked around the room—it was small, the décor authentic, as if they had stepped back into the nineteenth century—and then his eyes locked with hers.

They stood in silent communion, staring into each other's

faces. Derek saw his own confusion mirrored in Ginny, the feeling that they should know each other, but that neither of them knew why. They might have remained there for hours if Ginny had not turned away.

"Melville kept John from coming into the house, so the young soldier ran down to the street and called out for Abby." Ginny pointed to the corner window. "She threw back the drapes, opened the glass, and they talked for hours—like Romeo and Juliet."

Derek's eyes strayed around the room, noticing the flowers. There were vases on the dressers, on the bedside tables, all filled with brightly colored bouquets.

Ginny smiled. "Beautiful, aren't they?"

He nodded.

"Melville kept turning John away, but the soldier bought Abby flowers and paid local children to deliver them for him, to let her know that he still loved her, that he hadn't abandoned her." Ginny stepped across the room to the window, her breath fogging the cold glass as she continued. "They say Melville finally murdered him, down there on the street, shot him in the stomach. John died looking up at the house, at this window, forever denied his one true love."

"What about Abby? What happened to her?"

"She saw the whole thing. With her soldier gone, there was no point in living. She...she hung herself." Ginny pointed to the far side of the room; a closet door. "In there."

Despite his coat, gooseflesh erupted on Derek's arms and neck.

"It wasn't long before the stories started," she told him.

"People reported smelling flowers throughout the house, even in the middle of winter. Some claimed to have seen the girl standing here, gazing down at the street corner, still waiting for her soldier to return."

Her eyes lowered and her voice became distant.

"And then there are the noises."

"Noises?"

"From the closet, the sound of a hanging body swinging and slapping the walls: creak...thump...creak... thump.

"One of the owners grew so tired of hearing it, he actually boarded the closet up. It stayed that way for years, until the state bought the house and turned it into a museum."

Derek moved to the closet and opened it. A single bulb dangled on a cord, visible even in the gloom. He found a light switch and flicked it on. Round hatboxes sat on a shelf and empty hangers hung on the bar below. Apart from a few cobwebs, he saw nothing to inspire fear in anyone.

Ginny turned away from the window glass and said, "This house...you felt drawn to it, didn't you? —like you needed to be here?"

"Yes," he admitted, and it was as if a huge set of barbells lifted off his chest.

Ginny smiled. "Me too, like I'd been here before. Like I... Like I belonged here."

"So...what?" He closed the closet door and moved away from it. "You think we're supposed to *be* them, Abby and John, reincarnated or possessed or—?"

Ginny cut him off with her laughter. "Possessed?"

Derek smiled in spite of himself. "Sound's pretty crazy, doesn't it?"

She took a step toward him. "About as crazy as me asking a total stranger out on a date."

It's destiny, he thought dimly, surprised that the voice in his head was now his own.

"There's a restaurant just down the street," she told him, "Food & Friends. I have some work to do here, but if you'd like to get us a table, I can meet you there."

"I'd like that," he told her, his nervousness melting like frost before the dawn. "I'd like that a lot."

Derek followed Ginny down the stairs into the gift shop, then walked out into the cold. When he glanced back over his shoulder, he saw her standing at the window, smiling, a young woman looking at her soldier, her love.

He smiled back at her, then made his way down the path.

———

Ginny watched him walk away; each step remembered by the snow-covered trail. Cold seeped through the window glass into her bones. She shuddered, her smile withering like rose petals.

He will not set foot in this house again.

The declaration filled Ginny's inner ear; a stranger's voice, but she felt its anger and determination as if they were her own. She glanced over her shoulder, found the male portrait that hung above the fireplace. It stared back at her, into her, icy as the winter chill.

Ginny walked to the register, to the drawer hidden beneath.

Her fingers slid inside, crawled through the darkness like a hungry spider, and when they found the .38-caliber pistol hidden within, they seized it.

He will not come near my niece.

She marched outside and hunted the soldier into the night.

THE GROVE

J oel wished he had the courage to kill the witch, to choke the life from her with his bare hands. He'd dreamed of doing it, oh yes, countless times, and those fierce visions brought him more joy than he cared to admit; his fingers wrapped around her alabaster throat until she stopped struggling and lay there, just as limp and motionless as she'd been on their wedding night. He wished he had the balls to do it for real, to snap her neck like a rotten stick and bury her in this garden, her moldering bones forgotten beneath a rainbow shroud of carnations.

At this point, it would be totally justified.

More importantly, perhaps most importantly, it would finally be over. He would be free.

The winding gravel path crunched beneath his leather shoes. White patches of Japanese iris bloomed on his right, while to his left, a yellow blanket of Gaillardias spread out across low lying hills. Summers kiss, they were commonly called.

He thought about Cathy, about the way she had kissed him before he had walked out the door. It hadn't been the quick peck she normally gave him. No, there had been urgency to it, genuine passion, and when she had pulled away, she had told him, "No matter what happens, know that I love you."

In his thirty-eight years, Joel had never fallen this hard for anyone, and the thought of a future with Cathy—someone he really cared about, someone who cared just as much for him—provided him the courage he needed to face the witch one last time.

Multi-colored Hydrangea and lavender Hostas gave way to blood red "ace of spaces," to a white stipplework of flowering spurge, but Joel did not pause to admire their beauty. No. The sooner this place was in his rearview mirror, the happier he would be.

He was halfway beneath a rose-covered arbor when he saw the witch seated at a black, wrought iron table, surrounded by a grove of exotic-looking trees with twisted, scaly trunks. Miranda. His wife.

God, it felt so wrong to still have to call her that.

Even before they were legally separated, they had lived separate lives. When Joel woke each morning, Miranda's side of the bed would already be cold. He'd find her out here, toiling in the earth as if her life depended on it, caring more for these damned plants than she ever had for him.

Now, a wide-rimmed sunhat shaded her face, and her dress was a loud, floral print, as if she wanted to appear part of her precious foliage. She sipped herbal tea from an antique china cup, waiting for him to take his place in the empty chair across from her.

He paused in mid-step, a manila envelope clutched firmly against his chest like a shield. *I should have brought my attorney along,* he thought, *to hell with what she said on the phone.* But it was too late for that now. He took a deep breath and walked over to the table.

Miranda looked up from her tea, and a little light flickered on in her dark green eyes, a spark of joy, of yearning. She grinned, her perfect teeth straight and even as a strand of pearls. Her face was just as flawless, no wrinkles, no blemishes; with a Romanesque nose, and bright red hair that spilled over her shoulders like molten lava.

There was an old saying about beauty being skin-deep. Joel never really understood it until he married Miranda.

"Darling," she said. She liked to use words like "dear" and "darling," but they held no affection. On the contrary, Miranda used "dear" or "darling" to mean stupid or inferior, and so she used the terms frequently with anyone and everyone who was not her. "You came."

"Did I have a choice?"

"You don't need me." Her eyes lowered to the envelope he carried. "A judge can grant you a divorce even without my signature."

"That would drag things out."

"Yes, it would." The corners of her mouth curled up slowly, reminding Joel of the Grinch. She made a big show of looking behind him. "Where's your little whore?"

"That's enough."

Miranda blinked; her smile widened. "Oh, I'm sorry, darling. I forgot I was speaking of the woman you love."

"Yes."

"And you never loved me, did you?"

No, he hadn't, at least not in the way that he loved Cathy. He had cared for Miranda, however, until it became apparent that they wanted different things. Joel wanted to be an equal partner in their relationship; Miranda wanted a lapdog.

He exhaled loudly and rolled his eyes to the sky. "If this is what you meant by 'hearing you out,' I'll be on my way, and *you* can—"

She held up her hand, still smiling, voice as amiable as ever. "My dear, you can't blame me for being just a little bit bitter about the whole situation, now can you?"

He wanted to say, *Yes. Yes, I* can *blame you. You're a stubborn, spoiled, conceited, manipulative little bitch who wants it all...everything...and doesn't give a shit who she has to hurt to get it, or keep it. None of which changes the fact that our marriage is over, and it has been for years.* But he didn't utter a word. Cathy had warned him not to get into a screaming match with Miranda, not to give the woman ammunition that could be used against them. And so he held his tongue and took his seat at the garden table.

Miranda sipped more tea and held out her left hand, her fingers wagging. She still wore her wedding ring.

Joel frowned. He handed her the manila envelope, watched as she opened it and let a thick bundle of legal documents slide out onto the table with a thud. He thought briefly of informing her that there were copies, in case she had a sudden urge to hold a lighter to them, but again, he remained silent.

She read the first page, then paused a moment to lift the small ceramic teapot; topped off her own cup and filled one for Joel.

He pushed the china away. "No thanks."

Miranda threw back her head and laughed, that horrible, high-pitched cackle of hers. Joel couldn't believe he'd once found it cute. "It's not poison, silly," she told him. "In Japan, they always celebrate with tea."

"We're not in Japan."

"Yes, but you are celebrating, aren't you?" She set the teapot down and flipped to another page of the sheaf. "Really, dear, I'm surprised Miss Minami hasn't performed a proper Japanese tea ceremony for you."

"Cathy's Korean. And, frankly, what we do or don't do is none of your damn business."

Miranda said nothing. She sat there, lips curled up in that horribly wide, Grinchy grin; sipped her tea and continued to read the documents, or pretended to read them.

A butterfly landed on the table between them, and Cathy's face fluttered once more to the front of Joel's mind. He thought of marrying her, having the family Miranda had denied him because she couldn't be "bothered" with children. It was all there, almost within his grasp.

He reached into his jacket pocket. "I have a pen."

Miranda giggled and he glowered at her.

"All in good time." She took another leisurely sip of tea, licked her lips, and said, "I want to make certain everything is in order, darling, read all the fine print. This house and these grounds have been in my family for generations. I'd hate to think I would unwittingly sign anything away. I'm sure you understand."

Joel tossed his pen onto the table. The wrought iron grill caught it like a fly in a web. Startled, the butterfly took flight, headed off toward the ugly, misshapen trees. "This isn't a community property state, Miranda. You can keep your big house, these grounds...all your holdings. I'm not asking for any kind of spousal support from you. I don't want anything but your signature."

"And you'll get it, dear," she assured him, a sharp edge cutting through her jovial tone. "When I'm ready, and not before."

"I can wait," Joel told her, barely holding his anger in check. "I've got nowhere else to go today."

He stood, grabbed the teacup Miranda had filled for him, and turned away. He couldn't stand the sight of her. Of course, the grove was not much of an improvement.

Joel had always hated these trees, with their crooked trunks, hunched and deformed. Their bark was slate gray; cracked, bumpy and uneven; crocodile skin. And while a lush curtain of leaves hung down from their upper branches, the lower limbs were completely naked, with ends that curled into tight spirals, like New Year's Eve noisemakers, or whips ready to snap. How Miranda could sit out here, day after day, and look at them, he would never know.

He sipped his tea, which was overly sweet, and caught sight of the butterfly again. It danced across the leaves, bright wings making it conspicuous; red sails on a green sea. Joel hoped it would lay eggs, leave behind an army of hungry caterpillars who would devour the grove whole.

Something shot out from beneath the green canopy. It snatched the butterfly from the air, reeled it into the shadows. A long, sticky tongue.

The tea caught in Joel's throat and he coughed some of it back into his cup.

"You all right?" Miranda asked behind him.

"Fine." His eyes were huge, staring. *Some kind of frog,* he told himself, stepping discreetly toward the edge of the grove. *Or maybe a lizard.* He wiped his lips with his hand. His own tongue felt thick, pasty. He ran it over the roof of his mouth, over the backs of his teeth.

"You're right," Miranda admitted, flipping pages. "This arrangement seems more than fair."

"Yes." Joel now stood poised next to one of the misshapen trunks. Slowly, he reached out. *Will it leap at me? Probably not. More likely, it'll scurry away as soon as the light hits it.* He grabbed a fistful of hanging leaves, lifted them like a veil.

A face stared back at him from the tree, eyes as red and as plump as two ripe berries, but it was not a frog, nor a lizard, and, even though it had the same gray pallor, the same cracked, scaly texture as the surrounding bark, it took Joel a moment to realize it was actually a part of the living wood. Then its brittle lips parted, revealing rows of needle-sharp thorns—

Teeth. The damn tree's got teeth.

—that snapped at his fingers as if they were prey.

Joel let go of the branches and his teacup and leapt back. The leaves fell neatly into place, hid the monstrosity from his eyes, but there was nothing to erase it from his mind. He blinked twice, scanned the neighboring trees, and saw similar faces on them as well. They were—

"My husbands."

He spun to look at Miranda, and the world spun with him. "Your—?"

She stood and dropped the papers, let them fall to the grass, then she took off her sunhat and tossed it aside like a Frisbee. "At one time or another, they all wanted to leave me."

It was getting dark. The sky, so bright and blue a moment ago, had clouded over, a spring storm rolling in. Joel tried to take a step but the ground tilted beneath his feet. He stumbled; fell to his knees.

"This garden is their home now," Miranda told him as she unzipped her dress; it slid down her legs, covered her feet in a printed bouquet. "And they'll never leave it."

Joel's tongue felt huge, his lips numb. He was drowning. His limbs felt like lead weights, dragging him down. *The tea...drugged?*

She took a step toward him. Naked. Her skin appeared fluid; it moved over her body in bands, like rivers flowing in opposite directions. "Neither will you."

The trees. Unnatural. Unholy. They seemed to move, to close in on him. Their branches uncurled, stretched and waved, grew longer, merged with the clouds.

Then sleep.

————

He dreamed of a woman who ripped off his clothes and tossed them. Joel smiled, but it faded quickly. This woman wasn't Cathy. This woman was older, with long, white hair that broke over her face in a frozen wave.

Cathy...

Sharp claws bit into his shoulders like fishing hooks, drew blood as they dragged him across the dewy grass. They pulled him into a deep hole, a grave. Damp, worm-ridden soil pushed in on him, imprisoned him.

No, he cried, over and over again, *Don't...bury me...Cathy...*

But this woman wasn't Cathy. This woman was elderly, with flesh that slumped from her bones like melted candlewax. She poured water over him, washed the blood and dirt from his face.

Cathy...baby...

No. This woman wasn't Cathy. This woman was ancient, with lips like dried rose petals. She sang to him; a soothing, Celtic lullaby, but the words were unintelligible, foreign— Gaelic, or maybe Latin, or perhaps it was all just the gibberish of dreams.

———

Joel opened his eyes and was greeted by a bright flare of sunlight. He squinted, momentarily blinded, but grateful. He'd been convinced he would find only darkness on the other side of his eyelids, that he had been buried alive. *A nightmare*, he thought, realizing how crazy it all seemed now: Miranda...the old woman... *the trees...*

But then why did he still have the odd taste of that tea in his mouth?

His eyes widened, adjusted to the light, and saw an all-too-familiar sight. Miranda. She knelt in a flowerbed, pulling weeds out by their roots. A horrid thought bobbed to the surface of Joel's groggy mind: his time with Cathy had been nothing but a fantasy, and this was still his life.

Then he noticed Miranda wearing the same floral dress, the same sunhat. And, by the length of the shadows, he could tell it was not morning but late afternoon. Sitting here, waiting for her signature, had he become so bored that he had dozed off in his chair?

Miranda looked up from her labor, flashed that unpleasant grin. "You're awake."

Joel attempted to turn his head, to look around, but his muscles were numb, useless. He struggled to stir his arms, his legs, to wiggle any of his fingers and toes, but none would obey his commands. He searched for his voice and found a hoarse imitation, "I—I can't move."

"Yes, dear, I know." She did not endeavor to help him, however, just tossed the weeds into a large metal bucket on the ground beside her, then wiped the sweat from her forehead. "You'll be weak for some time, I'm afraid. But don't worry, it will pass."

More thoughts surfaced in Joel's mind, visions from the dark depths reserved solely for terrors too horrible to contemplate. He felt his eyes widen. At least he could still feel that. "What have you done?"

"Magic," she said, then waved a soiled hand through the air

as if she were conducting some symphony. "Flesh is such a wonderful medium, so malleable."

Joel's panic grew. His eyes rolled in their sockets, strained to see what lay at the outer limits of sight. His arms...they were there, held up in surrender, in a mockery of crucifixion. Shackled to one of the trees? No. The thin branches he saw sprouted from his own forearms, birthed through slits in his skin.

Look at my skin!

It had become gangrenous—dark, mottled, and crusty. He wanted to shake his head, but couldn't, wanted to deny this as the aftereffects of whatever drug Miranda had slipped into his tea, but, somehow, he knew that it wasn't.

He was staring at the trees again, uncertain of when his gaze had shifted, staring at their trunks with rancid fascination; his entire world, everything he held true, collapsing beneath the weight of the unimaginable. They were men, or at least they had been, men like himself, with fears and desires just as strong and as deep as his own. And like them, he was now trapped, a prisoner in his own flesh, becoming something abhorrent, with no clue to a means of escape.

The realization threatened to send Joel's mind reeling toward cliffs of lunacy, but he was quick to take the reins and haul it back. He drew in a long, trembling breath, held it, and tried to relax.

I have to stay calm...have to focus, to think!

Miranda reached into her metal bucket and produced a dead squirrel. She stood up, holding the animal by its fat, bushy tail. Its legs were outstretched, stiff. She grabbed one and peeled it from the carcass.

"Hungry?" she asked a nearby tree, then stuffed the squirrel's limb into its waiting mouth.

It gnawed on the leg with obvious satisfaction.

Joel felt his stomach roll.

Miranda looked over at him. "They eat anything really; insects, birds, raccoons...oh, and possums, they do love their possums. Sometimes, I even offer them special treats."

"Stop...Jesus..." He closed his eyes and ran his tongue over his lips; they were dry, lumpy and cracked. "I get it, all right! You want to punish me, but—"

"I don't want to punish you, darling. I want to save you."

His eyes snapped open again, glaring. "From what?"

"From yourself." She ripped off a second furry limb and popped it into another tree's mouth. "I can give you everything you need—"

"I don't need *you.*"

"Well, now you do." The remaining legs were fed to a third and fourth tree. "I'm going to take care of you. I love you."

"You don't know what love is," he growled at her. "You haven't got a fucking clue."

"Oh, but I do, dear." Miranda walked over to him, the limb-less squirrel dangling from her fingers like a furry snake. "I could have killed you, Joel. Easily. And instead, I gave you a new life." She grinned. "You may even decide you like it better than your old one."

"You're crazy."

Miranda giggled at that. "No, darling, as you are so fond of pointing out, I'm a witch." She held the squirrel closer. "Hungry?"

"Get that thing away from me!"

"Suit yourself." She tossed the carcass back into her bucket, then moved off toward the house; left him alone.

No. Joel knew he was far from alone. A cabal of tree-men stood all around him, their perverse trunks an omen of his own inevitable fate.

"Bullshit," Joel said aloud. He was not going to accept this. Miranda was not going to win.

He gave his arms and legs another mental tug. Then another. And still another.

In his mind's eye, he saw Cathy come home to an empty apartment. She would stand at the window, waiting for his car to pull in. Pacing, frantic, she would call his cell phone, the office, getting no answer, wondering where he was.

"I'm stuck here, baby," he whispered to the grove. "But I'm trying to get home. I really am."

He concentrated, fought harder to wiggle his fingers and toes, labored to twist his torso, to tilt his shoulders or turn his head. But, despite all his grunting and straining, he moved nothing; he felt nothing.

An hour became two, then three. Shadows grew longer; light dimmed along with his hopes. Then exhaustion crept over him, and the more he wrestled with it, the stronger it became.

Finally, sometime after dark, Joel lost the fight.

————

The old woman came unbidden once more to his dreams. She danced through a benighted grove; wearing not a stitch of clothing, loose skin flapping and swaying with every leap and bow, white hair pinwheeling. Her waltz ended at one of the trees—

Men!

—where she rubbed her sex against the bark like a bitch in heat.

Tightly coiled limbs unfurled as if they longed for her touch, then swelled and stiffened within the woman's ancient grasp. She straddled them; petrified branches slid between doughy thighs, gave attention to long barren terrain. Green leaves and white hair ruffled in the breeze as the old woman wrapped herself around each misshapen trunk, impaled herself again and again, all the while, moaning and howling in ecstasy.

Joel wanted desperately to be made blind. But no matter how hard he fought, how fervently he begged, the dream would not permit him to close his eyes. And when it finally allowed him to at least look away, it conspired with the moon to keep him a voyeur, projecting an obscene shadow play upon the lawn.

Stop! Please...stop!

And after a time, it did stop, the lascivious noises replaced by playful laughter. The old woman moved across the grove toward him. Her deeply furrowed skin, now slick with sweat, shone in the moonlight. Leaves and bits of moss clung to her, and here and there—on her bulbous, sagging breasts and boney hips—dirt was streaked like war paint.

She stood in front of Joel, her face emaciated, the face of a mummy fresh from the tomb. Her eyes were huge, black pupils rimmed in yellow, an owl's eyes. She ran a dry, blistered tongue over withered lips and reached out for Joel; her hooked, scaly hands ended in sharpened talons, calling to mind a bird of prey.

"Stay away," he pleaded, and the sound of his own dismal voice made him shudder. "Leave me alone."

The hag suddenly transformed. White hair turned black, silken; her skin was made supple, golden. Flaccid breasts lifted and blossomed, and those eyes, so huge and round before, became narrow, angled up.

Joel stared at the vision in disbelief. "Cathy?"

Her finger touched his lips, fine and smooth. "It's alright. I'm here now. I'll make everything better."

And it was better. Her full, moist lips met his, and all of his fears melted away. He felt her warmth, her hands working against his length, and he could not help but be aroused.

Cathy folded her arms around him, stared lovingly into his eyes as she mounted him.

"I love you," he told her while they coupled, over and over again, "I love you."

Cathy grinned and moaned, and when she climaxed, her screams turned to laughter, a horrible, high-pitched cackle that left Joel feeling cold and hollow inside.

———

He awoke to the sound of distant voices. Instantly alert, he strained to see where they were coming from. And, though he was still unable to move, at least now he could feel. Strange sensations. Wind whispered through a canopy of leaves that was now a part of him, teased branches that were an extension of his own limbs. And something crawled up what used to be his right leg, tickled him, an ant, a spider or a fly; he could not see what it was, nor could he brush it off.

There came a crunch of shoes on the garden path, growing closer, near enough now that Joel could make out what was being said. And though he was not mentioned by name, he knew that he was the topic of conversation.

Miranda asked, "Did you see his car in the drive when you pulled up?"

"No," someone replied.

Then Miranda said, "Well, I can show you the garage, dear, if you'd like, but I assure you, the man's not here. At least, not anymore."

The police, he thought, allowing himself a brief moment of hope. *When I didn't come home, Cathy called them, told them I was on my way here when she saw me last, and right now, some wonderful beat cop or detective is questioning Miranda.*

Salvation was just on the other side of the grove. All Joel had to do was call out to it, make his presence known, then they would see—

What? he wondered. *Will they be able to tell it's me? Is there any part of me that is even recognizable as human anymore?* And, most importantly, even if they found him, even if they knew exactly who he was: *Can any of it be undone? Can they make me* me *again?*

Joel didn't know, but he knew he had to try. He opened his mouth and closed his eyes, prayed he would be heard when he shouted, "It's me! I'm here! Help! Please, help me!"

Running on the gravel now.

It worked! They're coming! He opened his eyes again and saw—

Cathy.

No dream. Not this time. She stood there in the center of the grove, stared at him, her brown eyes wide with shock, her hands pressed over her mouth.

"Oh Jesus," she cried through splayed fingers, unable to suppress her revulsion at the sight of him.

She's going to turn away! his mind screamed. *She's going to run home and never look back.*

But instead, Cathy stood her ground and asked, "Joel? My God, is it you?"

Somehow, she could recognize him. Somehow, she *knew*. Perhaps his assessment of the situation had been far too gloomy. The transformation was not yet complete; there was still hope.

"Yes," he told her. "It's me."

"How?"

"I don't know. Please, don't leave me here."

"Never." Cathy took a step toward him, tears threatening her eyes, her hands and lips trembling. "Never."

Joel was so fixed on Cathy that he didn't notice Miranda, at first, carrying a shovel into the grove, a spade caked with dried dirt and grass, perhaps the very shovel she had used to dig the hole he was planted in. She held it up like a baseball bat and aimed for Cathy's head.

"Behind—!"

But it was already too late. Miranda swung with all her might; metal met the back of Cathy's skull with a loud *CLANG* that propelled her to the ground.

"NO!" Joel shrieked, but there was no denying it. The woman he loved lay just out of sight, just out of reach. He strained to move, to act, but his feet were rooted to the ground, his arms stiff as boards. He felt what must have been his lower branches; they uncoiled like tentacles, stretched outward, but they could not touch Cathy, could do nothing to pull her out of harm's way.

Miranda glanced up at him, and Joel was seized by indescribable terror. Her beauty melted away before his eyes, left behind the old woman from his dreams; her shriveled lips peeled back to reveal a skeletal grin. The hag straddled Cathy, held the shovel up high above her head, then slapped it down hard.

Joel heard the sickening crunch of bone, felt warmth splatter across his body.

Blood.

Cathy's blood.

He saw it dot the crone's dried up face. Dark red syrup. Drops of it clung to the white tangles of her hair; they ran down the strands and fell like rain.

The hag's yellow-rimmed eyes glowed brightly even in daylight. She tossed the bloodied shovel aside, reached down with those hooked talons of hers, and the grove echoed with a hellish chorus of wet rending sounds.

Joel wanted to close his eyes, knowing that, if this were a dream, it would not be permitted. If it were a dream, he would be forced to bear witness to this desecration. Then, when he finally woke up, the old crone would be gone and Cathy would be alive and well, somewhere safe, somewhere far from here. But his eyes *did* close, and even in the dark, he could hear the moist rip of Cathy's flesh as it came unanchored from her bones.

Cathy!

Every dream shattered with her skull. Everything that brought him happiness in this world, washed away in a tide of blood.

When Joel allowed his eyes to open once more, the hag was gone and Miranda stood in her place, her arms slimed red up to her elbows, glistening chunks of meat dangling from each hand.

"Here." She shoved the raw flesh at him. "You need to keep up your strength."

He slammed his mouth shut, made certain that none of the meat could touch his tongue.

Miranda smeared the slick chunks across his lips, glossed them scarlet. "Come on now, open up. I'm sure you've eaten Miss Minami before."

Joel glared at her, a soup of fury and frustration coming to boil.

"Oh, I'm sorry, darling." She frowned, her voice dripping with fraudulent guilt. "I forgot...it's none of my business what you did."

Miranda laughed merrily, a lunatic's laugh, but Joel knew she was far from crazy. No. She was evil—a demon freed from the bowels of Hell itself. She took the bits of flesh away from his lips and moved on to neighboring trees; eager creatures whose thorny fangs took the morsels off her hands, then licked her fingers clean with their long, sinewy tongues.

Numb, Joel lowered his eyes, tried to catch a glimpse of Cathy's body, but she remained beyond the reach of his sight.

Perhaps that was for the best. *At least it was over quickly*, he told himself, trying to find comfort. *At least Miranda can't make* her *into a monster. Or can she?*

Joel turned back to Miranda, watched as she spun the dial on a garden spigot, ran her arms through the fountain, and turned clear water crimson.

"What are you going to do with the rest of her?" he asked, feeling cold inside.

Miranda shrugged. "I'll take any leftovers and scatter them into the sea." She looked over at him. "Won't be the first time."

"She would've called the police."

"She did. But you're an adult, dear, not a child. You haven't even been gone a full twenty-four hours yet, and when they wouldn't let her file an official missing person's report, she went out looking for you herself." Miranda grabbed a metal watering can, filled it. "You signed the divorce papers...I signed the divorce papers. They'll get filed, I assure you, and then, if anyone bothers to ask, I'll say you ran off to Mexico with your whore. End of story."

By the tone of her voice, Joel could tell that she'd planned this from the beginning. He labored to count the other trees in the grove, stopped at a dozen, but there were still more. How long has she been getting away with this?

"People can't just disappear," he warned her. "No calls on our cell phones, no charges on our credit cards...they will know something's not right."

Miranda carried the full watering can over and knelt down. Joel could hear her riffling through something, and when she stood again, Miranda held up a Visa card, Cathy's face smiling at him from the picture on the back. Then, before his eyes, she *became* Cathy. Red hair dyed black as her soul; pale skin molded into shape by unseen hands and tinted gold. "Who says there won't be any more charges?"

The sight of that twisted grin hung on Cathy's face, corrupting her beauty, was an affront that Joel could not let stand. "Take it off!" he spat at her, eyes steely despite his tears. "Take it off right now, Goddammit!"

Miranda laughed at his pain. "It's not a suit, darling. Besides —" She licked Cathy's lips. "—you seemed to enjoy it well enough last night."

Joel frowned. Whatever string held his innards together was suddenly cut, allowing everything to come uncoiled. It wasn't a dream: Miranda, the old woman, this doppelganger of Cathy that now stood before him...all the same wretched creature. How could he have let it touch him like that? How could he have thought it was Cathy?

"What happens now?" he asked, feeling vile, humiliated.

The witch took another step forward, put Miranda's face back on, but even this look was counterfeit. Was this the hag in her youth, or beauty stolen from someone else—perhaps the love of another man, a man she had imprisoned here in the grove? And when she came to him at night, was he still aware of the withered horror that lurked beneath this mask? Or was he so far gone that he now believed only in the dream?

"You can grow and thrive, like the others," she told him. "You can live on for a hundred years or more, if it suits you."

Miranda stepped closer to him still. She reached out and her fingers skidded across the rough surface of his bark, wiped away his tears. Joel let out a disgusted hiss, as if a rat had just brushed his cheek.

"Or," she went on, "you can allow yourself to wither away; a few weeks, a few months, however long it takes for you to die. It's entirely up to you."

Life or death, it all seemed so pointless to him now. Cathy was gone. No matter what he decided, there was nothing that would bring her back.

But Miranda could still *use* her.

Joel thought of this crone slipping back into Cathy's form; thought of her using it to seduce a stranger down the aisle, a man who would grow to despise the real Miranda as all men who came before him had grown to despise her; a man who, sooner or later, would wind up planted here.

And then, Joel remembered another dream, an older dream; a fierce vision that brought him even more joy now than it had then—fingers wrapped around Miranda's alabaster throat, snapping her neck like a rotten stick.

He could do it now.

Easily.

Joel glared at her through the green, leafy veil that threatened to cover his face.

"I'll grow like a weed," he told her, "choke out everything else in this damned garden, and then, *darling*, I'm going to choke the life out of *you*."

Miranda smiled. She tipped her watering can, soaked his thickening roots; her eyes never left his. "Bring it on."

SANDWALKERS

S and. Sand was the enemy. It gummed up chopper motors, turned fierce war birds into flightless metal hulks. It jammed M-16s, left deadly weapons nothing more than impotent weight, left soldiers defenseless in battle. And, when propelled by Afghanistan's merciless wind, it scoured body armor and skin alike.

Foster wore the same armor and helmet as the Marines he now shadowed through this sandstorm, but he didn't belong to their ranks. The soldiers of Bravo Company knew it the moment they laid eyes on him back at the outpost. They saw his Nikons, saw the hardshell cases for his video gear and his Macbook Pro slung over his shoulders, and their heads wagged. Matching body armor or no matching body armor, journalists stood out like a sore thumb and made easy targets for Taliban snipers.

In previous wars, reporters were viewed as non-combatants, no different from unarmed civilians. Sure, covering the front lines was dangerous work, and of course there were casualties, but they were few and far between. In war, however, things change rapidly, and rarely for the better. Journalists were now viewed as a cog in the American military's propaganda machine, and, as such, they were fair game.

Sand collected around the edges of Foster's ballistic goggles. He pressed his handkerchief firmly against his nose and mouth. The Marines' weapon-mounted lights were now barely visible through the gritty murk ahead.

Foster quickened his pace, tried not to lose sight of the shadowy figure in front of him; the holstered .45 that hung from his belt hammered his hip with each hurried step. He knew these sandstorms could develop without warning, but he'd never seen anything like this. He'd watched dust clouds bubble up, forming a mountain on the horizon—a churning mass that rolled toward Bravo Company like a wave and swallowed them whole.

"Where's this village?" Master Sergeant Conlin yelled, his voice nearly lost to the wind's roar. "We need shelter fast!"

Another voice called out from the veil, "Just ahead, sir!"

Was that Corporal Ross? Yes, had to be. He was on point.

In moments, structures loomed out of the sand like a gothic citadel. The Marines hugged a stone wall, proceeded with caution; they didn't expect to dodge sniper fire in this storm, just as they didn't expect the town elders to form a welcoming committee, but they weren't taking any chances.

Wooden poles materialized—a framework for awnings. Tarps, ripped from their moorings, now flapped in the gale like tattered flags. Foster noticed they were not traditional Afghan colors. No. They were red and white, the motif of Arab insurgents.

Corporal Ross noticed it too. He ducked beneath these tarps and swept their path with his eyes, leveling the barrel of his M2. Nicknamed "Ma Deuce," the heavy machine gun was his best friend in-theater. He found a locked entrance and motioned them forward.

"McBride," Conlin called. "You're up!"

Private McBride spoke both major Afghan languages: Dari and Pashto. He put his gun aside and knocked on the door, shouting greetings in both tongues.

No response.

"Try Arabic!" Corporal Miller chimed in. His eyes moved from those tattered tarps to Conlin. "Want me to break it down, Sarge?"

"Move on," Conlin ordered. "Look sharp, people!"

The Marines resumed their march. They strode single file, weapon-mounted lights illuminating their immediate surroundings and little else. The opposite side of the street was a specter in the sand.

As they moved deeper into the village, Foster was reminded of a Wild West ghost town. Wind howled between scattered brick structures, buffeting Bravo Company with grit and bits of trash. An old-fashioned motorcycle lay riderless on its side in the dirt street. A propane tank sat on one end of a vendor's make-shift scale, but the other side, now full of sand, weighed more. A metal sign rattled with every gust. But there were no goats, no dogs, and no people. No signs of life at—

"Jesus!" Miller called out. "Would you look at this shit?"

Foster glanced over and saw the severed head of a camel. It was tied to a post along their walkway, swinging in the wind like a piñata. Blood dripped from its ragged stump, splattering dirty steps below. Its eyes were wide, and its tongue hung out like a wolf in one of those old Tex Avery cartoons.

"Sick fucks," Miller concluded, his eyes locked with the animal's glassy stare. "Probably the village elder's ride. Cock-suckers cut off its head as a warning."

"Wound's too jagged," Corporal Harrison corrected. Bravo Company's medic approached with care, sensing a possible trap; his eyes darted between this mutilation and the sandy void beyond. He touched the bloodied stump with his gun barrel, spun it around to get a better look. "This baby was ripped off, not cut off."

Foster reached for his Nikon and snapped a quick photo. Soldiers spun instinctively toward the flash. Miller aimed his rifle squarely at Foster's chest. The journalist lifted his hands in surrender, the Nikon swinging from his neck on its strap.

Miller glared at him. "Fuckin' shutter bug."

"Save it," Conlin snapped. "Let's move."

"Sure thing, Sarge." Miller backed away, but his weapon never lowered.

Foster hesitated, then followed along with his companions, feeling more isolated, more alone, than ever before. The wind whistled its happy tune, taunting him. He glanced back over his shoulder and saw that the post had already been swallowed up by the blowing sand, taking the bloody camel head with it.

Ross slowed as another entrance came into view; he nodded to his right and McBride moved quickly to flank him. Conlin crouched at the door; the knob turned easily and a gust of wind pushed it in.

McBride shouted bilingual greetings, waited, then said, "Nobody's home."

"Nobody's answering. There's a difference." Conlin peered into silent darkness, then eased out of the way and motioned Ross forward.

The corporal stepped in, "Ma Deuce" preceding him through the door. He illuminated every dark corner, eyes and weapon moving in unison, trigger finger ready. Nothing rose up out of the shadows to challenge him, however.

"Clear!"

Conlin led them into shelter. McBride and Harrison were right behind him. Foster was last, accompanied by Miller who closed and bolted the door behind them, blocking out the wind.

In the glow of their Surefire lights, Foster saw evidence of a struggle. Chairs and tables overturned. Ceramic bowls strewn over dusty floorboards, some already shattered, others breaking beneath the soldier's boots. And, most disconcerting, dark stains on the walls. Foster didn't need to be a medic to know they were dried blood.

McBride saw it too. "Merry fuckin' Christmas."

Foster nodded, surprised that he'd nearly forgotten the date. That was the angle of his piece, after all: how these men coped with being separated from their families during the holidays. Now, he didn't know what his story was.

If the others noticed the blood and shambles, they gave no indication. Miller remained on guard by the door with his shouldered M-16. Ross stationed himself on the opposite end of the mess, "Ma Deuce" still at the ready; his hulking frame filled a darkened archway that led to the next room. Harrison flanked him, his eyes on Conlin, waiting for orders; he didn't have to wait long.

"Don't get comfortable, people," the master sergeant cautioned. "Give me a sweep. If there's so much as a flea in this motherfucker, I wanna know."

They went into the next room, the Marines' movements as choreographed and precise as a ballet, though Foster thought these battle-hardened warriors might take offense at the comparison. Foster's gaze darted left then right, following the lights projected from their weapons and wishing for his own set of night-vision goggles. There wasn't much to find in this modest dwelling, and what little there was had been ransacked. A few pictures hung on the walls, their glass cracked, their frames askew. Long pillows were scattered about, torn open and bleeding stuffing. Hand-woven rugs that once covered the wooden floor lay bunched up to one side, as if something had been dragged across them. And, of course, there was more blood; it decorated the walls like modern art and streaked the naked floorboards.

There had been a massacre here. That much was clear. But there were no bodies. No bullet holes. No signs of explosives or—

Ross held up his hand.

The Marines stopped, listened.

And then Foster heard it too. Rapid breathing. At first, he thought it was the sound of his own nervous respiration, but no. They were not alone in the room.

The soldiers whirled around, their lights spearing a floral-printed sheet that hung on the far wall. Ross pointed, took a step toward it. McBride nodded, covering him.

Foster felt his entire body tense. Writers had active imaginations, and right now, his was feeding him every conceivable horror that might be lurking behind that curtain. His hand left his Nikon, traveled down to his belt; he popped the snap on his holster, ready to draw his .45 with the speed of a gunslinger.

Ross reached out, curled his fingers around the edge of the curtain, then yanked it aside.

Two Afghan children cowered from the light, a girl and a boy. They were filthy, emaciated, their eyes just as wide and staring as the camel's that hung outside, but they were alive. The girl was a teenager, covered in a long, brightly colored dress that was now smudged and torn. Dark hair trailed from beneath her tattered head scarf, hiding half her face. Tears had cleared lines in the dirt on her exposed cheek. The boy was much younger, perhaps six or seven, and his once white clothes were covered in so much blood that they now appeared tie-dyed in the light.

The girl held up her hands and said two words in perfect English.

"Don't shoot."

———

Outside, the wind roared and howled like an animal. It hammered the stone walls with dirt and sand, creating a sound akin to frenzied scratching. And it pushed on the door, demanding to be let in, whining its frustration through the cracks.

Foster righted an overturned chair and sat down. He emptied sand and pebbles from his boots, watching the Marines, who were intent on their duties. Ross and Miller stood sentry, weapons still at the ready, refusing to stand down even though the building had been cleared. Conlin sat at a nearby table with his hand-held radio, searched for an active frequency, but so far, only found static. Across the room, McBride and Harrison put their guns aside and bent down to work with the children.

The girl poured out her frantic tale in Dari or Pashto, but "don't shoot" appeared to be the only English she knew.

Foster found that sad.

The boy hadn't uttered a word in any language. He sat with his chin on his knees and stared blankly off into space, a blood pressure cuff wrapped firmly around his filthy arm. Harrison modified it to fit the boy's smaller limb, and Foster could tell this wasn't the first time the medic had checked a child's vitals.

Conlin looked up from his radio, frustrated. "What's she saying over there, Private?"

"She's in shock, Sarge," McBride told him.

"If I wanted her medical condition, I'd ask Harrison. I need to know what the hell happened here."

"She—" The private stood, frowned. "She says it was Sand-walkers."

Conlin blinked at him.

At the door, Miller burst out laughing and shook his head in disbelief.

"First," McBride continued, "they got the goats, got the horses and the camels, then they came back for the villagers."

Foster's eyes darted between the three men. "What's a 'Sandwalker?'"

"It's bullshit, Shutter Bug," Miller answered with his usual eloquence. "A fuckin' fairytale."

McBride shrugged and gave a more helpful, albeit less believable response, "It's another name for a Manticore, like a...a distant cousin to the Sphinx: body of a lion, bat wings, with a man's face and a scorpion's tail."

Miller chuckled and cracked, "Sounds like the date Harrison took to prom."

No one else laughed.

But it *was* ridiculous, the very idea that this carnage was the result of a rampage by mythical desert chimeras. Some insecure part of Foster's mind even considered that it might all be a joke the Marines were playing on him. After all, none of them were crazy about having a journalist tag along. And Marines all stuck together, didn't they—Semper Fi, and all that?

Conlin scowled as if he'd somehow heard Foster's thoughts. "All right, people. Obviously, the girl's seen some traumatic shit."

"I think they both have." Harrison removed the blood pressure cuff and packed up his gear. "They're also hot, hungry, and dehydrated, which is a good cocktail for hallucinations."

The master sergeant gave a disappointed nod; he took his hands off the radio, surveyed the faces of his men. "Okay, here's the facts. We've got to assume that whoever did this is still in the area. We're cut off, and we won't be able to establish a satellite link until this storm dies down. Even if we could, no chopper's gonna swoop down and extract us, and no predator drone's gonna give us any useful intel, not in this shit. So we've got to do what we do best: watch each other's backs." He took a pack of cigarettes from his breast pocket and slid one between his lips; it bobbed up and down as he spoke. "That's the bad news."

"What's the good news?" Foster asked, unnerved.

"The good news?" Conlin lit up, inhaled deeply, then exhaled like a steam engine ready to blow; the smoke swirled around his helmet, glowing in the weapon-mounted lights like a halo. "For the moment, the building's secure, and the storm should pin the bad guys down the same way we're pinned down." He pointed at Foster with his smoldering cigarette, emphasizing every word. "They can't *hit* us if they can't get *to* us."

Foster nodded. Looking at the children, however, at the blood they'd bathed in, he felt little comfort, even in this tight knot of well-armed warriors. "How long do sandstorms usually last?"

"Depends."

"On what?"

Conlin blew more smoke. "On if it's a *Haboob* or a *Shamal*."

"What's the difference?"

"*Haboobs* die down in a few hours. *Shamals* can go on for days."

The Afghan girl tugged on McBride's uniform and started in again. Her eyes were not as manic as they had been before, but they were no less haunted. In fact, she seemed quite anxious about something.

"What's she going on about, Private?" Conlin wanted to know.

McBride held up his hand, listening to the girl's harried rambling, making certain he heard every nuance and his translation was accurate. "She says that we can't stay here. She says it's not safe."

"No shit," Ross growled softly, his powerful machine gun cradled in his muscular arms.

"If we don't leave right now," McBride continued, "the Sand-walkers will kill us the same way they killed her parents and her other brothers and sisters."

"You and your brother have got nothin' to worry about, little lady." Miller stepped forward, smiled confidently. "Me and my squad here have fought monsters before, and this—" He presented his M-16; the barrel was pointed away from her, but she recoiled against the back of the chair as if squarely in its crosshairs. "—will put their dicks in the dirt before they can even lay a hand on you."

Realizing she couldn't understand a word of it, he glanced up at McBride.

"Go on, tell her not to worry. Tell her she dances with total fucking bad-asses."

The private almost certainly paraphrased, but the girl seemed to grasp the sentiment, even if she didn't find it as reassuring as Miller intended. She relaxed a bit in her chair and hugged her brother to her side, combing his disheveled hair with her fingers. Her troubled eyes drifted slowly to the door and never left.

———

Foster's Swedish grandmother once told him that the Sandman was a diminutive creature in a very long nightcap, a helpful little sprite who carried a huge sack full of magic sand over his tiny shoulder. If you were good all day long, so her story went, the Sandman crept into your room late at night and sprinkled some of that sand into your eyes. This was supposed to put you into a deep, untroubled slumber where nothing awaited you but the most pleasant and wonderful of dreams.

It was an innocent fairy tale, told with love and affection, but even as a child, Foster found it all quite sinister. He'd have nightmares about a horrible little troll who snuck into his bed at night, cackling as it emptied its entire sack over his face until he suffocated beneath the weight of a huge mound of sand. And when he awoke, Foster found grit still lodged in the corners of his eyes, evidence that he was lucky to have survived to see another dawn.

Now, as he watched these Afghan children drift off to sleep, their angelic faces covered over in blood and very real sand, Foster was reminded of innocence corrupted. And as he looked over at Conlin and McBride, napping in chairs with their helmets pulled down over their faces, he thought of the horrors witnessed by an entire generation of young men and women, and he wondered if any of them would ever have pleasant dreams again.

Harrison plucked a deck of cards from his pocket and invited Foster to a friendly game of poker. The journalist was eager to oblige. He welcomed any distraction from these blood-stained walls, from the incessant drone of that damned wind outside.

"You have any family back home, Corporal?" Foster asked.

The medic shuffled his deck. "This for your story?"

Foster blinked. "Just making small talk."

Harrison dealt cards and said, "I've got a wife and a six-year-old boy. She was supposed to buy him this remote control Iron Man figure for Christmas. She wanted to say it was from Santa, but I told her, 'Hell no! You put "From Daddy" on that one!'" He chuckled ruefully, then glanced at his watch and considered the time difference. "He's probably opened it by now. I can't wait to see the pictures."

The journalist fanned out his cards without looking at them. "Must suck, missing out on so much?"

From the doorway where he still stood watch with Ross, Miller sneered. "Do they actually teach a class in stupid questions at journalism school?"

"What's your problem, Miller? I'm here to tell *your* story, to help you—"

"Bullshit!" the corporal spat, then he looked over at the sleeping Afghan children and lowered his voice. "You're here to *steal* our story and make it yours, to help nobody but yourself. See, I know all about you."

"Is that so? Enlighten me."

"A Marine's on trial right now for fucking war crimes because of pricks like you," Miller accused. "He finished off some wounded asshole down in Fallujah, some insurgent that had been killin' his friends all day long, and if the tables were turned, would've drug him off and decapitated him live on the fucking web. Was he the only one to do it? Hell no. He was just the only sorry sonofabitch to get caught on tape."

The corporal pointed at his own helmet.

"And you people...do you even take a second to *think* about the effect a video like that's gonna have? Hell no! All you think about is your fucking ratings and the fact that you just got the scoop on everybody else. Now, that crap's all over the damn net for any suicide bomber to see and *we're* the ones here with targets on our backs." Miller sounded more frustrated than angry now; he sat at the table across from them and placed the butt of his M-16 against the wood. "So, while we're fighting these fuckers the best way we know how, you're taking pictures for the enemy's recruitment posters. *That's* my problem."

"I see." Foster gave a single, slow nod. "Well, I don't pretend to know anything about you, Miller, but—" He pointed to the Afghan girl. "—I saw the way you acted with her, and I got the feeling that you might actually be an okay guy."

Harrison smiled into his cards before he caught himself, but Miller didn't notice. Miller's eyes were locked with Foster's.

"And when you told her that you fought monsters, I actually believed you," the journalist said, and he meant it. "I believed you because you're right; anybody who kills men, women, and children for shock value is about as evil a creature as I can think of. *My* problem is that terrorists don't have a monopoly on evil. See, in my world, monsters don't just come in one shape, size, religion, or uniform. So, you fight them your way—" He nodded at Miller's M-16, then held up his Nikon. "—and I'll fight them mine. But, since neither one of *us* is a monster, there should be no reason why we can't do our jobs without pissing in each other's canteens."

They regarded each other for a moment, neither one blinking.

Harrison spoke up, anxious to change the subject. "So are we going to play poker, or what?"

"You guys can play if you want to," Miller told them. "I got work to do."

And with that, the corporal stood and took up his position at the door.

Harrison leaned across the table as if to share a secret. "Don't let Miller get to you. He's a little more gung-ho than some, but I trust him with my life, and so should you."

"I trust all of you." Foster shifted in his chair. "And before this is over, I hope you'll trust me."

Miller eyed the journalist with skepticism. "We'll see how you do in a fire fight. If it comes to—"

"Quiet," Ross called out, and their eyes shot to him. "Listen!"

Miller cocked his head to the left for a moment, then shrugged. "I don't hear anything."

Ross nodded. "Exactly."

And then it hit them all in the same instant.

The winds had stopped.

————

Silence met Conlin's preliminary requests for evac, but the sergeant kept at it, and in time, his determination was rewarded with a static-laced female voice. "Move... four...the terrain to...extraction."

"Say again? All after 'move?'"

She repeated, much clearer this time. "Move approximately four kilometers farther up the terrain to a hilltop for dawn extraction. Over."

"Copy that. Bravo Company over and out." Conlin holstered his radio, stood and pointed to the sleeping children. "McBride, explain it to 'em."

The private gave a quick salute and obediently crossed the room. When he nudged the Afghan girl, her eyes snapped open and she recoiled into her chair with a guttural moan. McBride held his up his hands as if to surrender, then spoke a few soft words. Whatever they were, she nodded her agreement, then woke her brother and repeated them to him.

"Ross," Conlin called, but his eyes were on the door. "You're on point. And Miller—"

"Rear guard, yes sir." The corporal smiled. "Don't worry, top, I got your back."

"Then let's move."

"What about me?" Foster asked, feeling invisible again.

"What about you?" the sergeant responded.

"Is there something I can do?"

"You can keep up."

A thud. Foster flinched, looked up. Dust rained and stray bits of leaves and reeds drifted down from the thatched ceiling.

Something landed on the roof.

"What the fuck?" Miller wanted to know, his voice hushed, the barrel of his M-16 aimed at the rafters.

The Afghan girl shrieked. She scooped up her brother, took off for the far corner of the room and hunkered down, tried to make herself as small as possible. Her brother's arms were locked around her neck, his face buried in her tattered headscarf; he sobbed and called out words that made no sense to Foster's ears.

From the roof came an answering cry; a symphony warming up—brass and woodwind sections playing different songs at the same time. It was as deafening as it was alien.

McBride ran after the children and whatever was on the roof moved with him. Foster heard it shift, heard it claw at the surface coating of plastered straw. And the wooden rafters cracked beneath the excess weight, cracked right above McBride's head.

"Look out!" Foster called.

McBride flashed his light around just as the flimsy ceiling collapsed. Splintered beams struck him square in his helmet. He went down hard, buried beneath split slats and reeds, beneath leaves and mud, beneath—

Foster staggered back wide-eyed, unable to believe what he saw.

Perched atop the debris was a winged nightmare. It landed on all fours in a supportive crouch like a cat. A very *big* cat. Leathery wings spread wide, flapped, then folded neatly over its hunched back. It paused—red, malignant eyes glaring; bits of the roof still stuck in its dark, unkempt mane—and then it took a step toward the Afghan children with one menacing talon. Its tail swung behind it, flogging fallen rafters; not a lion's tail, Foster noticed, but the segmented appendage of a scorpion.

The journalist stood there, one hand on his camera and the other on his gun, poised to shoot the thing one way or the other, yet unable to move. Beside him was Conlin. The sergeant had no doubt seen much in his tours of duty, but it was obvious that he'd never seen anything like this.

"Real," he muttered aloud, his voice low and hoarse. "God...*damn.*"

The Manticore took another step forward, smooth muscles flexing beneath its pelt, membranous wings fluttering. Its tail now stood erect, swaying back and forth like a cobra ready to strike; there was something at the tip of it, something razor sharp that gleamed in the lights. Those red eyes narrowed and its lips parted with a silky purr, revealing rows of triangular teeth. Shark's teeth.

Miller bared his own teeth and uttered a snarl of primal anger. He thrust the barrel of his M-16 toward the thing and opened fire. Flowers of blood bloomed and wilted across the creature's side in rapid succession. Its purring turned to a loud, cacophonous screech that once more reminded Foster of a symphony in need of a conductor.

The Manticore spread its wings and flapped them, fanning dust and debris. Foster couldn't tell if it were attempting to take flight or simply trying to shield itself from Miller's projectiles. It succeeded in neither.

At that point, Ross stepped forward, opened up with "Ma Deuce," and it was all over. Massive shells reduced the creature's head to shrapnel. The Manticore collapsed on a death bed of fallen roofing, tattered wings enfolding its corpse like a bloody shroud.

Harrison pushed past them. He slung his rifle, knelt at the rubble, and dug frantically for McBride. Miller followed his lead, glancing up through the jagged hole in the ceiling with increasing regularity, clearly waiting for more creatures to poke their heads through.

Another thud on the roof, this time over the back room where they'd found the children. Foster flinched and spun toward the darkened archway. Ross took aim. From his kneeling position, Miller joined him. Harrison paid no notice and kept right on burrowing with his hands.

A hand slapped Foster's back. Conlin. "Get 'em," he shouted and pointed.

Foster ran to the Afghans. He grabbed the girl by her elbow and pulled her up to her feet. She drew away, clutching her brother tightly to her breast, dampening his hair with her tears.

"It's okay," the journalist said. He wrapped his arm around her waist and shoveled her across the room. "We're going to be all right." He knew she didn't understand a word of it, but he said it anyway. Perhaps he just needed to hear it himself.

"Marines," Conlin called as he backed away, aiming his rifle past Foster and into the dark.

"We're not leavin' a man behind, Sarge," Miller replied, covering Harrison. The medic continued to dig.

In the next room, the roof gave way. Sounds of splintering boards joined that horrible symphony of a Manticore cry. The thing was inside.

"Got him," Harrison announced. He pulled an arm from the debris, gave it a tug, then turned to Miller. "Help me!"

Keeping his M-16 on the archway, Miller reached down with one hand, grabbed a fistful of McBride's uniform and helped yank his comrade free.

Conlin nodded in relief. "Is he—?"

"He's alive, Sarge," Harrison said, two fingers on McBride's neck. Then they dragged his unconscious body across the floor, backed rapidly toward the entrance; Harrison used both hands while Miller's right arm still held the rifle. Then the Manticore pounced on them.

Foster never heard it make a sound, and its speed was incredible. It seemed to materialize in mid leap. Its fur was a maroon blur in the lights, the same color as dried blood, and its teeth were white as Christmas snow.

Miller instinctively pulled his trigger, but by then the thing's jaws had closed around McBride's torso and it wrenched the body from their grasps. Wings fanned out and flapped, and the thing swooped up through the hole in the ceiling its twin had made with McBride still in its mouth. Its long, segmented scorpion's tail snaked through the air like a streamer and was gone.

"McBride!" Miller screamed, and then he fired another futile volley of shells into the night sky. "Mother-fuckers!"

Sergeant Conlin turned his attention to the entrance, fumbled with the knob. The door was barely open a crack when two sets of talons pushed through. Foster's heart stopped, and in his arms, the Afghan girl screamed.

Ross muttered a curse and spun toward the door just as the creature wedged it open and slammed Conlin against the wall. The corporal pulled his trigger and unleashed Hell, sending the thing's shattered skull flying backward, fountaining blood. Their path was now clear.

The sergeant stumbled to his feet and managed to get enough wind back in his lungs to yell commands, "Let's go, people! Go now! Go, go, go!"

They ran out into the night.

———

Ross sprinted up the walkway, "Ma Deuce" laying down an uninterrupted field of fire. Foster and the Afghan children hadn't even cleared the doorway before he'd cut down another beast with his shells. He pivoted left, then right, searching for his next target. There was a screeching roar as it found him instead.

The Manticore charged out from an alley; it leapt on Ross' back and knocked him off the walk. He landed face-first in the sand, the creature straddling him. Ross didn't scream or call out in any way. He didn't have the time. The beast decapitated him with its jaws, then spit his helmeted head into the street like a peach pit.

Miller walked toward the Manticore with his M-16, casually firing as he moved. Blood splattered from its body and it let out a shriek that rang through Foster's skull like cathedral bells. It hopped off Ross' spurting corpse, spread its wings and soared.

Behind them, another Manticore leapt at Corporal Harrison. The creature's tail whipped around, and its knife-like tip skidded across his chest armor in a burst of sparks. The corporal drew his rifle, but before he could fire off a shot, the stinger lashed out again and buried itself in his face, cleaving his skull in two. He was lifted off the walkway and flung aside.

Jesus! Foster's mind cried, as if the word were magic, as if uttering it on this night would make all these horrible visions go away. *They're everywhere! How many can there be?*

The Manticore pounced on what remained of Harrison, who'd been good with children and wanted nothing more than to see pictures of his own son's Christmas joy. Wings extended from its lean body and it took triumphant flight, its kill dangling from between its pointed teeth. Blood fell like hot rain as it passed overhead, sprinkling the walkway and the sandy street beyond.

All this happened in the space of a minute. Then Conlin plucked the radio from his vest and screamed into it. "Dust Off Fifteen, we have a nine-line in progress!"

Foster pressed himself flat against the stone wall, still holding the sobbing Afghan girl around the waist. He suddenly realized that he didn't even know her name. Her brother let go of her neck and clamped his hands over his tiny ears, trying to block out the sounds of Miller's gunfire.

In front of them, Conlin was still on the radio, relaying their location, their casualties, and stressing that a firefight was in progress. He did not, however, share any details about *what* they were fighting. Something sharp burst from his throat in a glut of blood, spearing his radio and ending the conversation—a Manticore stinger, driven straight through his neck from behind.

The beast turned its attention to Foster and the children. It glared at them, narrow red eyes burning with hunger. And when it flicked its tail, Conlin's head came unhinged from his falling body.

Foster instinctively reached for his camera; it came to whirring life in his hands, creating a rapid *click-click-click* and a series of brilliant flashes. In that harsh, artificial light, he got his first good look at the Manticore's hideous face. The myth claimed it to be that of a man, but nothing could've been further from the truth. The nose was triangular, flat and flayed, bat-like, and its skin was as dark and wrinkled as a raisin.

Blinded, the Manticore screeched and turned away, turned right into Miller's line of fire.

"Eat shit, Fuckface!" the corporal shouted, pulling back on his trigger.

A volley of shells opened that horrid face. One of the creature's eyes exploded and it rolled off the walkway, collapsed in the sand, blood spreading out from beneath its body in a dark, viscous pool. Another Manticore swooped down and grabbed it up. Perhaps they were cannibalistic, or maybe they had their own rule about never leaving a comrade behind.

Foster scanned the walkway and the street beyond. Sergeant Conlin's body was gone as well. So were Ross and the other dead Manticore. Puddles, streaks, and splatters of blood were the only evidence that they had ever existed at all.

———————

Miller sat on the edge of the walkway, staring out across the sand toward the rising sun. "When that chopper comes, you get the kids outta here."

"What about you?"

The corporal answered Foster's question with a question. "Why'd those things bug out of here so fast?"

"I don't know." And he didn't care. They'd left them alone, left them alive. That was enough. "Animals can sense things people can't. Maybe they can hear the chopper coming, maybe they think it's bringing reinforcements."

"Or maybe they knew it was dawn."

Foster shrugged. "Maybe."

"They all flew off in that direction." Miller nodded at the mountains on the horizon. "There's caves up there, miles of 'em. Dark places where they can hide from the wind and the sun, maybe even from God Himself. Anyway, it's just an educated guess, but I gotta start somewhere."

Foster gaped at him. "You're not going after them?"

"Somebody has to."

"By yourself? That's crazy!"

"I don't expect you to understand."

"Good, because I don't." Foster held up his Nikon. "I've got pictures, Miller. Proof. Like you said, we shoot this stuff, put it on the web, and it goes viral. When they see these things, they'll have to—"

"You fight the monsters your way, and I'll fight them mine." Miller gave his rifle a loving pat, as if it were his faithful dog, then he lifted his gaze to meet Foster's unbelieving stare. "They were my family, Shutter. The only one I've ever had. I owe it to 'em, to *their* families, to find 'em and bring 'em home."

The journalist opened his mouth to say something else, anything that would dissuade Miller from this insanity. And then a terrible, insufferable picture developed in his mind. Harrison's wife and six-year-old boy, standing over an open grave, over an empty casket, never knowing where the man they loved had gone, never having the chance to say good-bye.

Foster shook his head, denying the image. He stepped off the walk, stood for a moment in the hot desert sun, then shaded his eyes with his hands. "You'll die out here."

The corporal shrugged. "Marines die every day, Shutter." He stroked the barrel of his M-16. "But before I go, I'm takin' the rest of those bastards with me." For a moment, he looked solemn —resigned to his fate, then he stood, smiled down at the journalist and said, "Don't you have to go write your story now?"

Foster shook his head and slowly backed away. "Their story, not mine."

"You know, Shutter," Miller chuckled, "I've got the feeling you might actually be an okay guy."

The corporal turned, stepped inside the open doorway, and kept out of sight.

Morning skies purred with powerful rotors. A Blackhawk helicopter. As Foster watched its sleek silhouette descend, exhaust blurring the bright orange dawn, he understood how the chopper earned its name. It swooped down just outside the village, landed with its twin engines still running, and waited.

The journalist relaxed a little, but not completely. He wouldn't relax completely until he was back at the fortified base, perhaps not even then. He looked over his shoulder.

The Afghan girl swayed on her feet, clearly exhausted, but still managing to hold onto her sleeping brother. Foster reached out and pried the boy from her arms. She didn't want to give him up at first, but the journalist smiled at her, let her know that everything was going to be fine now, and she offered a tentative grin of thanks in return.

Together, they hurried to the waiting chopper and never looked back.

————

From the shadows, Miller watched them go, then he glanced down at the weapon in his hands.

"This is my rifle," the corporal said aloud. "There are many like it, but this one is mine."

He took the handkerchief from around his neck and wiped the barrel.

"I will keep my rifle clean and ready, even as I am clean and ready. We will become part of each other."

When the sound of rotors faded, he stepped out onto the walkway and turned his eyes back to the desert, to the distant mountains beyond.

"Before God, I swear this creed. My rifle and I are the defenders of my country. We are the masters of our enemy. We are the saviors of our life."

He upended his canteen against his lips, drained it dry, then tossed it aside.

"So be it, until victory is America's and there is no more enemy."

Miller leveled his M-16 and walked out across the sand.

IN VINO VERITAS (WRITTEN WITH TIM WAGGONER)

"Something about this doesn't feel right, Eliot."

I looked over at Bill Gardner. He was Native American – what we called *Indian* back then. He was oldest of us, in his fifties, but he was still in fine shape for his age. A good man to have at your side when things got rough, which they did all too often.

"It's not like you to spook, Bill."

We sat in a black sedan parked on the street in one of the less reputable suburbs of Chicago. It had snowed last night, just a dusting, but the white stuff did nothing to class the place up. This area was lousy with gambling joints and whorehouses – and speakeasies, of course. That's why we'd come here: to raid a speakeasy. But we weren't here to bust down the door of some run-of-the-mill Juice Joint. We'd gotten word that this place was special. *Very* special.

Bill sat behind the wheel of the sedan, I sat in the passenger seat, and Lyle and Paul sat in the back. We were waiting for the others to arrive. They were late, but not too late.

"I'm not spooked," Bill said.

Even though the engine was off, he kept his hands on the wheel. He stared through the windshield at the supposedly abandoned warehouse at the end of the block. The warehouse – or rather, what was inside it – was our target.

"A place like that is sure to be well protected," Bill said. "It's going to have steel doors for certain. So why didn't we bring The Truck?"

Capone was a smart sonofabitch. His speakeasies had reinforced steel doors as well as escape hatches for his customers. The lowlifes inside had plenty of time to get the hell out and scatter while agents tried to batter the steel door down with slegehammers. At least, that's the way it had been until I decided to fight steel with steel. The Truck had an arrow-shaped battering ram attached to the front, and once we started using it, the doors to Capone's speakeasies began falling like dominoes. No more hammers for us. But today we didn't have The Truck, and it was obviously making Bill nervous.

"We don't need it," I said. "In fact, if we tried to use it for this job, I guarantee you that not only wouldn't it work, it might get us all killed."

"What do you mean?" Lyle said. "Capone started booby-trapping the entrances to his joints? What's he using? Dynamite?"

Lyle Chapman was, among other things, a tactician, and I could practically hear the wheels whirring in his head as he thought.

"No booby traps, and no dynamite," I said. "What's inside

that place –" I nodded toward the warehouse – "is way worse than simple explosives."

"Do us a favor, huh, Eliot, and stop beating around the bush. Just tell us what's going on."

Paul Robsky was a short guy, average-looking, not one to stand out, but he was an expert at wire-tapping, and as good as he was at the mechanics of it, he was even better at the art of it. He knew how to listen – I mean, *really* listen. He could hear what people said, but more importantly, he heard what they *didn't* say. This skill was the main reason I'd brought him along today.

"Sorry, boys. I'm not trying to be a pill. But to be honest, I've heard some pretty wild stories about this particular speakeasy, and I'm not sure I believe them myself. If I filled you in on all the details, you wouldn't believe me. But I can tell you this much: if even half of what I've heard is true, this isn't going to be like any raid we've ever conducted before. So whatever happens, stay on your toes and take your cues from me. All right?"

Their scowls and mutters told me it damn well *wasn't* all right, but they weren't going to make an issue of it. I'd done right by them before, and they were going to stick with me. I just hoped this raid wasn't going to end up being our last.

A sedan came rolling down the street and parked directly behind us. The rest of the boys had arrived, and it was time to go to work.

"Okay," I said as I reached for the door and stepped out into the snow, "let's do some good."

The wind off the lake was frigid as ever, and I saw bits of ice sparkle in the faint light of the streetlamp on the corner. I opened my overcoat and slipped my revolver out from its shoulder holster, checking it yet again, drawing both comfort and courage from its familiar weight in my hand. If things went sour, I knew I could count on it, just as I knew I could count on my men.

Bill noted the lack of mobsters on guard as we approached the door to the warehouse. "Where's all the pearl gray hats?"

"Yeah," Lyle agreed. "What gives, Eliot? No pearl hats, no heaters...You sure the kid's not sending us on some wild goose chase?"

"The kid" was my nickname for Georgie Thomas, my best informant. He was on the fringes of Capone's organization, and eager to help in any way he could. In fact, I think he considered himself an honorary G-man, but I knew he was working both sides, so I took everything he said with a grain of salt.

"The kid's not the only one with a story about this place," I told them, and it was the God's honest truth. "Word on the street is they brew some kind of special hooch in here."

Special, I thought. *That's a good name for it all right. People go out looking for a good time, legal or not, and instead they wind up patients in Cook County Insane Asylum, clawing their own eyes out and licking the walls of a padded cell.*

But not everyone.

That was the really weird part about it. Some people drank the stuff, whatever it was, and they came away happier than they'd ever been in their whole lives. The kid's own wife, a burlesque queen who went by the name of Le Flame, even said she'd felt closer to God than she ever had in church. They liked the stuff, and what's worse, they wanted more.

Other people... *Capone's* people... they took one sip of the stuff and just went nuts. I heard one pearl hat, Eddie Aiello, ran screaming from this place like he was on fire, kept yelling that his skin was melting from his bones. He ran right out in front of an oncoming train, and after it smashed into him and dragged him the length of Wrigley Field, he finally stopped screaming.

"Just..." I took a deep breath, tried to calm myself, then I glanced back over my shoulder at the boys. "Keep your eyes and ears open."

They looked at one another. Billy's eyebrows rose, then he shrugged and said, "Sure thing, Eliot."

Paul stared at me for a moment, and I knew then that, despite my best efforts to hide it, he heard the nervousness in my voice. If he was concerned, however, he didn't let on. He just motioned toward the warehouse entrance. "Lead the way, boss."

I walked up to the door. It *seemed* unremarkable. I took a deep breath and knocked.

A panel slid aside, revealing a tiny window set into the wood. An eye suddenly filled the entire opening — huge, bulging — I figured the window had to be some kind of magnifying glass. And then we heard the voice; it was deep, guttural, almost like a growl, "Password?"

I swallowed hard and said the word that had been given to me, a word repeated again and again by the men who kept head-butting the walls at Cook County: "Olympia."

The eye disappeared, and the panel slid closed again. We stood there in the dark, in the cold. I began to wonder if the password had changed, or worse, if I'd been recognized, and then I heard the loud sound of metal locks being turned within.

Bright light outlined the entrance. As the door swung inward,

I got a good look at the doorman. When the kid told me this guy only had one eye, I was picturing someone wearing a black eyepatch, like a pirate. No. This man, this...*thing* had a single eye set right in the middle of its skull, a huge orb that now scanned each of our shocked faces.

I was beginning to understand why the kid had warned me not to use the Truck. *The place is protected by a hell of lot more than steel doors*, he'd said. *Only way you'll get in – and more importantly, get back out – is by using your melon.*

The doorman had long greasy black hair and a thick beard with bits of food stuck in it. He wore a tunic belted at the waist by a length of rope, and sandals with criss-crossing leather straps that went up to his knees. He was covered with body hair so thick, it almost qualified as fur, and his tunic was splotched with dark stains that I hoped had been caused by spilled wine. The Cyclops – because really, what else could he be? – stepped aside so we could enter, but now that we had permission to cross the threshold, I hesitated. A smell rolled over us, and it wasn't the usual speakeasy stink of alcohol, body odor, and stale cigarette and cigar smoke. The joint smelled of exotic spices and zoo animals, the odor so strong that it hit you like a slap in the face. I didn't hesitate because the smell was offensive. Quite the opposite: it was attractive, compelling, even. It called to something deep inside me, a part so ancient that it predated the concept of *human*. I didn't just want to go in; I wanted to *run*, and I could sense that the men behind me felt the same. But we weren't called the Untouchables for nothing. I took a deep breath, let it out, and then stepped inside. The others followed.

Most speakeasies weren't much to look at. People went to

them to soak in alcohol, not atmosphere. But the interior of this joint looked like the inside of a museum. The floor was made of marble, and columns lined the walls at regular intervals, or at least where walls should've been. Between the columns was empty space, and beyond them rolling green fields beneath an achingly blue sky. A gentle breeze blew from across those fields, a warm *spring* breeze. The columns supported a domed ceiling upon which was painted a scene of naked men and women engaged in revelry – dancing, laughing, singing, and screwing – all of them holding goblets filled with dark red wine. Some guzzled it, some poured it on each other, and some flung the contents into the air. They shared similar expressions of sheer ecstasy, and I wondered what it would be like to feel that way, even if only for a moment.

The chairs and tables looked more normal than the rest of the place, but they had been fashioned from expensive mahogany and polished to a high shine. The bar was made of the same material, with a gleaming brass rail and a long curving mirror mounted between the columns behind it. The mirror's frame looked like it was made of gold and encrusted with glittering jewels. It had to be fake, I told myself. Hell, this entire set-up had to be nothing more than an elaborate gag. But if that was true, then why did it feel so goddamned *real?*

The doorman wasn't the only bizarre-looking creature in the place. While there were plenty of human men and women in the joint, sitting at tables drinking and laughing, other . . . *things* were in attendance as well. A short skinny guy with curly brown hair, a scraggly goatee, pointed ears, and honest-to-God horns walked by on hairy goat legs, hooves clip-clopping on the marble floor. He carried a glass of wine, and as he took a sip, he gave me a wink, as if we shared some private joke. The . . . I struggled to remember the word . . . the *satyr* was naked, which provided an unfortunately unobstructed view of his long, thick penis. It wobbled as he walked, and I couldn't help being impressed, despite myself.

"Guy like that's bound to be popular with the ladies," Bill said.

The satyr's pointed ears twitched in our direction, and he called back over his shoulder, "More than a few of the gents, too!"

The bartender was equally naked, a muscular man with long, glossy black hair and a full beard. His features had a roughness to them, but he wasn't unhandsome. What he *was*, however, was a centaur. It took a lot of space behind the bar to accommodate the equine part of his body, and his horse tail swished back and forth as we entered. That, combined with the scowl on his face, was a clear sign that he wasn't happy to see us.

Paul noticed the centaur giving us the evil eye, and he said, "Screw you and the horse you rode in on, buddy." He paused, then added, "Wait a minute. That's you, too, isn't it?"

Some of the guys laughed nervously, but most kept mum as they looked around, struggling to reconcile what their senses were telling them with what they knew – or *believed* they knew – was reality. Me? I thought it was a pretty funny joke.

There were other creatures from myth in the place. A hodge-podge monster that was part lion, goat, and dragon – a chimera, I think it's called – lay on the floor, lapping wine from a crystal bowl, and a harpy crouched on top of a table, mottled jugs swaying as she took a sip of wine from an upside-down human skull and then began to preen her filthy, matted feathers. Another woman stood not far away from the harpy. She was beyond beautiful and naked, but much of her body – the best parts, anyway – was concealed by long bluish-white hair the color of ocean water and sea foam. She was playing a tune on a small harp with her delicate fingers and singing softly. It took me a moment to recognize the song: "Love Me or Leave Me." The siren's voice possessed an unearthly quality unlike anything I'd ever heard before or since, but I still prefer the Ruth Etting version of the tune.

But as strange as all of this was, there was something even more bizarre about the place. In the middle of the room was a table larger than the rest, around it a trio of luxurious high-backed leather chairs, two of which were occupied. One by a young man wearing a tux, and the other by the evil cocksucker himself.

Capone grinned, stood up, and spread his arms wide, as if delighted to see us.

"Glad you and your boys could make it, Ness!"

Billy, Paul and the others immediately reached for their revolvers. Every eye in the place, both human and monstrosity, suddenly focused on us. Giddy laughter turned to gasps. That harpy stopped preening her feathers and hissed. The chimera lifted its heads from its bowl and growled. Capone... Well, Capone was all smiles. In fact, that scar on his cheek made it look as if his grin went all the way up to his ear.

I held up my hands. "Now wait a minute, boys, there's no reason for things to get ugly."

"Look around, Eliot," Billy quipped. "This joint's got no shortage of ugly already."

"Just put the bean shooter away," I said, and then I turned on the rest of the boys. "That goes for all of you."

They were slow to lower their pistols, and I could practically see the gears turning in their heads, each of them trying to figure out what plan I had up my sleeve to get Capone, and more importantly, to get out of this crazy place in one piece. As I looked back at the table, I was trying desperately to come up with one.

The person sitting next to Capone was young, although I couldn't pin down his exact age. Late teens, maybe early twenties. He was male, I was fairly sure of that, but he was clean-shaven and had delicate, almost feminine features. His hair was jet-black and curly, and his eyes were a dark purplish color, although I figured that had to be a trick of the light. I mean, who has purple eyes? Then again, who has goat legs or half a horse's body? Compared to that, purple eyes didn't seem so strange.

He wore an expensive-looking, well-tailored tux that fit his lean body like a glove. In one hand he held a glass of red wine, while in the other he held a wooden rod covered in some kind of ivy – grapevine? – atop which was mounted a pine cone, of all things. The rod should've looked ridiculous, but the youth held it in an almost regal way, as if it were some sort of scepter. I had a hard time keeping my gaze focused on the damn thing. Looking at it for too long made my eyes hurt. It was like staring into the sun.

"Please, Mr. Ness," the young man began, and those odd eyes of his locked with my own. He motioned to the empty chair. "Do have a seat. I must admit, I've been quite anxious to meet you. I've heard so many *fascinating* tales."

His voice was a soft, mellow tenor, single-malt scotch mixed with freshly harvested honey. His words were warm in the ear, and hearing them felt like a shot of fine bourbon going down – smooth and warm, stimulating and relaxing at the same time, but with a bite to it as well. *Like life,* I thought, not entirely sure what I meant by that.

His movements were languid, almost sleepy, but his eyes were alive with keen intelligence, amusement, and something darker which I couldn't name.

I glanced back over my shoulder at the boys once more. They'd managed to put their pieces away, but their hands still lingered in their coats like a bunch of damn Napoleons. The kid's words were in my head again: *Use your melon... Only way you'll get in – and more importantly, get back out...* I nodded and made steps toward the vacant seat.

"Sure, what could it hurt?"

"Indeed," the youth said, his pale hand tightening around that ivy-covered scepter.

A trio of women stood behind him. They were dressed as flappers in short skirts and with bobbed hair, but the style didn't suit them. They were lean and muscular, and their faces exuded a cruel, almost malevolent beauty. Their features were sharp, their gazes feral. Their nails were long and bright red, and their lips were the same shade. The color reminded me of freshly spilled blood. Those lips drew back as I approached the table, the expression more of a snarl than a smile, revealing rows of sharpened teeth. I didn't know what they were, or what they might do to me and my men if I made the wrong move, and I hoped that I wouldn't find out.

I took my seat with deliberate slowness. Capone, the smug sonofabitch, adjusted his necktie, then did the same. All around us, the joint's clientele gradually lost interest, and the debauchery resumed.

"Now this is my kind o' place," Capone said with a grin. He took a swig of whiskey from the glass in front of him, then added, "I could become a regular."

The effeminate youth gave a regal nod in reply.

"From all I've heard about this place, I thought it would be, you know, more exclusive." I glanced over at Capone. "Turns out you'll let just about anyone in."

"Better watch your lip, treasury man," Capone said, still smiling, and then he nodded at his new friend. "You don't know who you're dealing with here."

The bastard had a point. Sure, I knew Capone had been the one to set this up. He'd fed the kid information, knowing it would find its way to my ear and draw us here. The kid was a two-way street, and I'd used him to give Capone false information more than a few times myself. But Al wasn't the one runnin' this show. It was Mr. Purple Peepers.

So, I asked him, "You got a name, friend?"

"I have several," he said, "but I prefer Dionysus."

He lifted his hand and snapped long, delicate fingers. One of the fanged women behind him — I had no idea what they were at the time, but I later learned they called 'em maenads — produced an ornate vessel. It was covered with ivy, like the guy's staff, and a crude drawing of a bull adorned its side.

"Allow me to offer you something to drink, Mr. Ness."

"I'll pass, thanks."

Capone laughed. "Against your religion?"

My eyes narrowed. "Against the law."

"The *law*." Dionysus shook his head, his smooth, effeminate features furrowing. "You gentlemen must realize this Prohibition of yours cannot hold. You, Mr. Ness, seek to deny mortals their passions, and you, Mr. Capone, seek to control who gets to embrace them, and under what terms. But nature cannot be *legislated*. It cannot be *contained*. And a flame, once lit, can never truly be snuffed. Zeus learned that lesson eons ago. That's why he never wanted your kind to have fire in the first place.

"How much fine liquor have you wasted over the years, Mr. Ness? — Just poured out into the ground for Hades to enjoy?"

I shrugged and nodded at Capone. "Why don't you ask him? I'm sure he's been keeping score."

The sonofabitch scowled at me. "You're Goddamn right I have been. You and your boys have cost me a fuckin' fortune."

"Thanks," Lyle chimed in from behind me. "We do our best."

Capone leaned back. "Just not good enough to put me out of business."

"Not yet," I agreed, "but evidently good enough to *scare* you."

Capone laughed. "Me, afraid of *you?*"

"Why else would you set up this little party?"

"Treasury man, you're nothin' but a badge and a whole lot o' talk."

"If that were true," Dionysus pointed out, "you wouldn't

have any issues paying your tributes, and you wouldn't need *me* to help you — How did you put it? — 'rub him out.'"

Capone got to his feet. "Listen, Nancy-boy, you're the one who wanted to meet Ness." He waved his hand at me. "Well, here he is. I brought him to you on a silver platter. Dig in! As for me and my crew, we're back to business as —"

"*Sit down*," Dionysus commanded. His voice was a good two to three octaves lower than it had been, almost like a growl, and he slapped his staff down on the table for emphasis.

Capone's fat face went slack, and he immediately took his seat — a puppy threatened by a rolled-up paper. I have to say, it made me smile to see it, but any little joy I had didn't last, because I knew that if a man like Capone was *that* scared of something, then it couldn't be good for any of us.

"I said that you could return to your pitiful little affairs only *after* the three of us had shared a drink." Dionysus reached over and took the decanter from the hands of his follower. "I'm sure you gentlemen have heard that I brew something quite special here."

"I have," I told him. "I've also seen what it does to people."

Some *people*, I reminded myself, *not everyone.*

"I call it Ambrosia," he said as he set the container down on the table between us, "the nectar of the gods."

"Is that what you gave my guys?" Capone asked. "Some kind o' weird moonshine?"

"Wine," Dionysus corrected, "The *purest* wine."

Another of the maenads brought over a tray of glasses — three, to be exact. She set them down in front of her master, and he uncorked the decanter, filling each one in turn.

"*En oinōi alētheia,*" Dionysus said as he poured, and his grin was more than a little seductive. "That's a very *old* Greek saying. Perhaps you gentlemen know it better in its Latin form? — *In vino veritas.* Either way, it simply means, 'In wine, there is truth.'" He looked me in the eye again. "The *ultimate* truth, Mr. Ness. You can put on a mask of righteousness —" And then he glanced over at Capone. "— give the impression of civility and sophistication, pretend to be something in public that behind closed doors you are not, but wine..." He finished pouring, then held one of the glasses up to the light. For a moment, the vintage actually seemed to glow, an inner radiance that was as beautiful as it was enticing. "...wine dissolves all those airs, drowns away all pretense, and what you are left with, my friends, is the reality of who you truly are."

He slid one of the glasses across the table to me.

"So, Mr. Ness...are you ready to meet the real you?"

I glanced down into the Ambrosia, my own face reflected as if in a pool of blood. It was the face of a good man, an honest man — a man who had sworn to do what was right. And yet, it was also the face of a man who'd lied to get what he needed, a man who'd *killed.*

"Don't do it, Eliot," Billy said.

"Yeah," Lyle agreed. "You don't know what's in that shit."

Capone's men all went mad. But I wasn't like them. Still...

I pushed the glass away. "Like I said before, I'll pass."

Dionysus frowned and those purple eyes of his seemed to darken. "I'm afraid I must insist."

And then, he brought in the muscle. I heard a loud snort and turned to see huge figures towering over the boys behind me —

giant, beefy men with the horned heads of bulls. Minotaurs. Their wet noses glistened and there was hot anger in their huge, brown eyes.

"They say your men are 'untouchable,'" Dionysus said. "That might be so in the mortal world, but here, in this place, I can assure you that it is not the case."

I glanced back down into the glass.

"Why?" I asked.

"Why? You've made liquor illegal, declared war against it, against *me*. The last person to do that was King Pentheus of Thebes. I made him drink too, made him take a good, long look at himself. He went quite mad. I certainly hope you fair better."

"If I drink this," I said, "no matter what happens to me, you'll let my boys walk out of here?"

Dionysus nodded.

It was then that someone put their hand on my shoulder and gave a slight squeeze. It was Paul. "Go on, boss," he said. "You'll do fine."

I wish I shared his confidence, his *faith*.

"Stupid prick," Capone chuckled. "That giggle juice is poison. You're gonna drop dead, Ness, or worse, wind up with bats in your belfry."

"You'd better hope not," I told him, staring at the remaining glass in front of Dionysus. "I'm pretty sure you're next."

I half-turned in my seat to look at my men. "So, what do you think?"

Lyle frowned as he thought. "We're all seeing the same things, so either we all went mad at the same time, or this is real. And if it is, then the only way to play this – maybe the only way for all of us to get out of this booby hatch alive – is for you to take that drink."

"*Feels* real," Bill said. "My ancestors believed there are many types of spirits in the world. Why shouldn't there be one in Chicago? But I'd think twice about taking that drink. Spirits have their own agendas, and they only tell the truth when it suits them."

"Dio-whatsis is hard to read," Paul said. "It's like his voice isn't really there, like I only *think* I hear it, if that makes any sense. Capone is easy, though. He believes all of this, *and* he's positive he's got you by the short and curlies."

No real help there, but I nodded to show I appreciated their advice anyway, and then I turned back around to face Dionysus and Capone. The choice was mine, and there was nothing to help me decide which way to jump. In the end, I think it came down to Capone and the smug smile on that sonofabitch's face. He thought he had me. Maybe I'd chicken out and refuse to take the drink, in which case he'd know I was yellow deep down, or maybe the booze would destroy my mind, and he'd be rid of me forever. Either way, he'd win. That's what he believed, anyway, which meant there was only one way I could beat him.

I locked gazes with Capone and smiled.

"Screw you, Al."

I took a deep breath, and then I drank.

You're going to think I *did* go nuts when I tell you this next part, but I didn't taste anything. I didn't feel any liquid touch my tongue or run down my throat as I swallowed. Instead, I *smelled* something: baking bread. My father was in the bakery business, and I used to help him out at work when I was young.

I'd always associated that smell with him, with home, with being part of a family, but most of all, with being loved. I learned responsibility in that bakery, along with respect, for myself as well as others. I learned the value of hard work there, and I also learned that something simple, like a fresh-baked cookie or a slice of cake, can help soften the rough edges of life, can bring people together and help them forget their troubles, if only for a short time. I understood then that alcohol wasn't any different when used right, and that was Dionysus' true gift to the world.

The full effect of the wine didn't last long, maybe a few seconds, but even after it faded, it was still there, just on the edge of perception. And I'll let you in on a little secret, kid. To this day, I can still bring that smell back full force whenever I want, still feel that same feelings inside. All I have to do is close my eyes and remember taking that drink.

My hand shook a little as I set my glass down, but when I spoke my voice was steady.

"Thank you," I said to Dionysus, and the god smiled and gave me a regal nod in return.

Capone leaned forward and squinted his eyes, waiting for me to exhibit the first signs of insanity. I just smiled at him, and after a minute he sat back in his chair with a sour look on his face and a muttered, "Fuck."

Dionysus slid the remaining glass over to Capone.

"Your turn."

Capone looked at the glass as if it held hydrochloric acid.

"Hell, no! I ain't touchin' that damn stuff!"

"The choice is of course yours," Dionysus said. "But if you

don't drink, I'm afraid I'll have to give you over to the less-than-tender mercies of my lovely companions."

The maenads moved behind Capone's chair and reached out with red nails that had lengthened into vicious claws. They bared teeth that were longer and sharper than they had been a moment ago, and as Capone tried to stand, they grabbed hold of him and shoved him back down. They held him there, and even though they were slender gals, no matter how hard Capone struggled, he couldn't break free of their grip.

"They like to tear things into very small pieces," Dionysus said. "It makes a terrible mess, but what can I do? I can't say no to the dear things."

Capone had looked scared before, but now he looked downright terrified. I wouldn't have been surprised if he pissed himself right there and then, and even though part of me felt a measure of satisfaction at seeing him humbled, another part of me – a bigger part – thought that no man deserved this.

"Does he really have to –"

Dionysus shot me a look, and I saw something in his eyes, a fierce coldness that wasn't even remotely human, and I shut my goddamned trap.

Capone looked at me then, his eyes pleading with me to do something, anything, but then his ego kicked into gear, and he realized he was asking his most hated enemy for help. The fear left his face and was replaced by an arrogant sneer.

"Fine. Sure. Why the hell not? I ain't got anything to be afraid of, right?"

Dionysus didn't say anything, but the maenads withdrew their crimson-clawed hands, and Capone leaned forward, took hold of the glass, and raised it to his lips. He took only the merest sip, and then he put the glass back down on the table. He sat still for a several moments, and I watched beads of sweat form on his forehead. Then, slowly, he smiled.

"See? Nothin' to it. I knew –" He broke off then, his eyes widening. At first I thought he was staring at me, but then I realized he was staring past me. Not at my men, but at something that wasn't there. Or maybe it *was* there, and the rest of us just couldn't see it.

"Clark?" Capone said. "Is that you? Naw, it can't be. You got yours on Valentine's Day!" He broke off, and his lower lip started to tremble. "Stop looking at me like that. Those eyes . . ."

He tried to turn away, but one of the maenads grabbed hold of his chin and forced him to keep looking.

Clark had to be James Clark, who Capone killed in the St. Valentine's Day Massacre. Was the man's spirit really there, staring at the bastard who'd gunned him down? Or was Capone seeing a ghost conjured by whatever atrophied remnant of human conscience he possessed? In the end, I suppose it didn't matter.

Capone tore free from the maenad's grip and rose from his chair. He tried to play it cool, but he got up a little too fast and lines of sweat ran down his face. He cleared his throat too loudly and adjusted his tie.

"That hootch didn't do nothing to me." He looked at Dionysus and his upper lip curled into a sneer. "Tasted like shit, too."

Dionysus merely smiled.

Capone turned to me then and fixed me with a steely glare.

"See you around, G-Man."

"Yes, you will."

I held his gaze for a long moment, and then he turned and started toward the exit, moving at a quick pace, as if he really wanted to run but didn't want anyone to know it. He looked back over his shoulder once. Not at me or Dionysus, though. He quickly turned back. The cyclops opened the door for him, and he rushed through without giving the one-eyed monster so much as a glance. It was over. Almost.

I looked at Dionysus.

"I don't see any reason to shut this place down. Not that I could," I quickly added. "Besides, I think it's a little outside my jurisdiction."

Dionysus looked at me for several moments, his gaze unreadable. But in the end, he smiled. "Go in peace, Eliot. You and your men."

I nodded then stood. Paul, Lyle, Bill, and the rest of the guys looked relieved, and I didn't blame them in the slightest. We all turned then and started toward the exit. The cyclops was still holding the door, and he grinned as we filed past. He gave me a fast one-eyed blink that I think was his version of wink, and I winked back. A thought occurred to me then, and just before I stepped back into what we mere mortals think of as the real world, I turned and called out to Dionysus.

"You know, I think Capone left without paying his tab."

Dionsyus' face was as impassive as that of a cold marble statue.

"Oh, we'll settle up later."

Capone was found guilty of tax evasion shortly after that. He spent years in solitary confinement, drowning in his own madness. From what I hear, he died still begging ol' Jimmy Clark for forgiveness.

And Dionysus? On the day the Volstead Act was repealed, ol' purple peepers sent me a package, an ivy-covered decanter of Ambrosia. Somewhere, maybe in a bar in some five-star resort hotel or maybe in a run-down roach-infested dive, I imagine he's sitting at a table, full glass in hand, laughing.

FOR THE RIVER IS WIDE AND THE GODS ARE HUNGRY

It was hot as Hell. No, hotter. And still no rain. Becky didn't think there had been as much as a drop in the last two months. The grass crunched like straw beneath her shoes and a few dry leaves rode the scorching August wind across her path.

Fed up and moving off to greener pastures, no doubt.

She saw a large, dusty boulder and sat on it, her knees crackling and popping like breakfast cereal despite her young age. She wiped her forehead with the back of her hand, her heart throbbing in time with her aching feet. "That's it. Stick a fork in me. I can't take another step."

Up ahead, her fiancé Mark put his hands on his knees. Sweat darkened his shirt and ran off the tip of his nose, sprinkling the thirsty ground. "Okay, sure." He tried to catch his breath. "We can take a break if you need one."

Becky chuckled. She took off her Nike baseball hat with the pink swoosh and fanned herself. "You're most kind."

They smiled at each other and he gave her a wink. Normally, they took their daily walks around Stanley University's campus track, their workouts in the air conditioned athletic center. But Mark had been dealing with her parents for a week now, and he was anxious to get out of that house. Truth be told, so was Becky. She'd gone off to an out-of-state college to get away from this place, after all. To escape. The only reason they were here now was because her mother refused to come to the wedding unless she met Mark first.

His head twitched suddenly to the right. "Listen to that."

And suddenly she heard it too. The sound of running water. Her stomach turned and a feeling of white-hot terror rose up the back of her throat like acid until she thought she might vomit or scream or both. For a moment, she hoped it was just the rustle of the wind through leaf-laden branches. But she was kidding herself. She knew it was really—

"The river!" Mark's smile widened; he seemed overjoyed.

She stopped fanning herself and the ball cap nearly slipped from her fingers. Her eyes moved uneasily to the tree line, visualizing the water that flowed just on the other side. How could they have come this close to it without her knowing?

Mark said something.

She blinked and her eyes shot back to him. "What?"

"I said let's go for a swim and cool off."

Becky recoiled as if he'd suggested murder. *"No."*

"Why not?"

"I didn't bring a suit."

"You don't need one," he said jovially. "There's nobody around for miles."

"No," she said again. "You *never* swim across the river during the Dog Days of Summer."

"You should hear yourself." He stood and chuckled. "You sounded like your mother just then, afraid of ghosts and her own shadow."

"Not ghosts," she told him. "I wish it was only ghosts."

"What then?" Mark wiped his face with his sweaty shirt and pointed to the trees and the water beyond. "Please, tell me why I can't go cool off in the nice river over there when it's a hundred frickin' degrees out here."

She chewed her lower lip, thinking it over, wondering just how crazy she would look in his eyes. "If I tell you," she began at last, "promise me you won't laugh, that you'll keep an open mind."

"I promise," he assured her, and then his hand traced an "X" through the air in front of his chest. "Cross my heart and hope to die."

Becky nodded and looked at the ball cap in her hands. She squeezed the bill so tightly that it bowed out of shape. "When...when it gets hot like this, the water belongs to...to *Uncegila*."

"Who?"

"*Uncegila*," she repeated, and just the sound of the name made her shudder despite the broiling heat. "The river serpent."

A laugh burst from Mark's lips, but the look in Becky's eyes killed it quickly.

"Do you want me to explain or not?"

"Sorry." He covered his mouth, embarrassed, then held up his palms and said, "Please, explain it to me."

She regarded him with a mix of hurt and skepticism, then began. "About ten years ago, I was out here with some friends. There was an old tractor tire tied to a big branch, and we loved to swing on it and then jump off into the water."

She glanced over at the trees with their dying leaves, wondering for a moment if the tire was still there, wondering how many kids had leapt from it over the years.

"Anyway, it'd been hot and dry all summer, and with no rain, there were warnings about lighting campfires and tossing cigarettes. We thought the river would've dried up to nothing, but it hadn't. It was still there, still flowing.

"It was me, and Jude Wilson, and his little brother Richie."

"You came up here alone with two boys?" There was a smile in Mark's voice.

She didn't smile back. "Turns out we weren't alone.

"We were standing at the river's edge, letting the water run over our feet. It felt so cold and so refreshing on that hot day." Becky didn't look at Mark, but she could tell that she wasn't helping her case, so she hurried on. "And then Johnny Sparrowhawk showed up. There's a Native American reservation on the other side of the mountain. We'd seen him around town, but we didn't go to school with him, even though we were the same age. The tribe had their own schools.

"Anyway, he hiked down the bank on the other side and just stood there...watching us.

"'You're not going in the water are you?' he called out, and he sounded just as scared as I did when you mentioned swimming to me.

"'Sure are,' Jude told him. 'Come on in.'

"And that's when Johnny told us the legend.

"'A century ago, when it got hot and dry like this,' he said, 'the tribe would ask their strongest young men to swim across the river to the other side. That's when *Uncegila* would come. She was a powerful serpent, just as long and winding as the river itself. She would come, and she would dine on the swimmers until she had her fill, and then, only then, would she allow the rains to return.'"

"And you believed him?" Mark asked.

"No." she told him, wishing they had. "No, we had a good laugh.

"'Don't say I didn't warn you,' Johnny said, and then he turned his back on us and hiked off toward the reservation.

"So Jude and Richie take their turns on the tire, swing out over the river and jump in. And they're out there, waiting for me, but I'm just standing there sweating in my swimsuit. I didn't want to admit it then, but Johnny's story had me more than a little creeped out.

"'Come on, Becky,' Jude kept calling.

"And then Richie, little Richie, who was barely out of the second grade, starts squawking and calling me chicken.

"So I backed up a few steps and was ready to take a running leap at that tire, when I saw something in the water."

"What kind of something?" Mark wanted to know.

Becky shook her head. For years, she'd tried to forget it all, to lock it all away, and now he was asking her to open the door to that vault and let the nightmares have free reign again. "I'm not sure exactly. It was *big*. I know that. It moved toward the boys, swam against the current, and it left a huge wake.

"And I couldn't say anything. That was the worst part of it. I couldn't move, I couldn't even scream. All I could do is stand there on the river bank; frozen, and mute, and forced to watch.

"I saw its head rear up, huge and scaly, and its mouth opened wide...so wide. Snakes can unhinge their jaws. Did you know that?

"Anyway, I remember it shrieked. I remember that *very* clearly. It shrieked, and the boys screamed, and then... then they were all gone. No Jude. No Richie. No serpent. I was all alone, and I was scared.

"And then these dark clouds rolled in. Storm clouds. It had been so long, I almost forgot what they looked like. The lightning flashed, and the thunder roared, and I didn't know what to do. So I ran all the way home in the rain and told my parents. I didn't tell them what I saw, just that the boys went into the river and they never came out. The whole town searched for days afterward, but they never found any bodies. They were just...they were gone.

"I haven't mentioned it or thought about it since, and I've never been back in that river. I never will go back. Never...*ever*."

She wiped a forming tear from her eye and looked up at Mark for the first time since she began. He stared back at her, and she could tell from the look in his eyes that he didn't buy a word of it.

He's going to laugh again. He's going to say, "I've never heard anything so ridiculous in all my life."

To his immense credit, Mark didn't do either of those things. Instead, he ran his fingers through his short-cropped hair and said simply, "That's some story."

"It's what happened," she told him. "It's the *truth*."

But I should've made something up, she thought. *I should've told him he couldn't swim because of chemicals, E. coli, something he would've* believed.

He held out his hand to her. "Come on. I'll walk over there with you and we can check it out together."

Becky shook her head adamantly. "No. I'm not going to go near it. I told you, I haven't been since, and I don't want to start now. Can't you see I'm scared out of my mind, Mark? Please, can't we just go back to the house?"

"I'm just going to go have a look at it." Mark pulled his sweaty shirt off over his head and backed toward the trees, the dry grass hissing with each shuffled step. "You can wait right here."

"No!"

"I'll just be a minute." And then he turned and ran for the river.

"Mark!" She stood and screamed after him. *"MARK, NO!"*

But he'd already disappeared over the rise.

Becky listened to the loose rocks along the bank slide and crunch beneath his sneakered feet. She knew what he was doing. He was trying to get her to run after him, trying to show her there was nothing to fear. But she couldn't run. She couldn't even move. Her feet were frozen in place, just like that day so many years ago...

No, no, no...Please...Not again...Please, don't let him—

A splash.

Oh God, he's done it! Oh Jesus, he's really gone and done it! Oooooh...

She sat down hard on the rock, white knuckled fists pressed firmly against her lips, and she waited to hear the serpent's unholy shriek, to hear Mark's dying scream. And when there was no shriek, no scream, no sound at all, she pressed her sweaty palms together in her lap, in silent prayer, and she waited for him to come back, to climb up over the rise, smiling and dripping and still laughing at her fears. She wanted that. She *needed* that. And so, with tears in her eyes, she waited and prayed.

And waited and prayed.

And waited.

And prayed.

And when dark storm clouds rolled in, and the scorching August sun slid for cover behind grateful trees, Becky found she had no tears left to shed. She prayed that the god was now satisfied, that it would allow her to stand, to *live*, and then she prayed that she still had the strength left to run.

Lightning forked across the sky in response.

Becky put on her cap, got to her feet, and ran all the way home in the rain.

MASAKO'S TALE

"Now, Momma, please?"

"Please, Momma?"

Over and over again.

"Please?"

Faint voices, no more than whispers; the roar of the waterfall outside threatened to drown them out entirely, but Masako heard each hunger-drenched word. She looked up, saw her children gathered around the hand-woven rug at the center of their shack; their tiny eyes glittered in the dimness, focused on the feast she'd laid out for them with great care, ready to devour it all.

"Not yet." Masako didn't like denying them, but this would not wait. "First, I must tell you something important."

She knelt down and gazed into their famished little faces, feeling so blessed, and yet, so dirty, so guilty, so *ashamed*.

"It's about your father," Masako told them, and then she looked away, searching for words.

A fretted lute, her *Biwa*, sat in the far corner of the shack, its strings calling out to her trembling fingers. Notes echoed through her mind, formed a tune, the tune she played the first time she saw him...

————

Masako sat on her front step, aware that there was a man watching her from across the lake. He was a very handsome man, naked but for the white *Mawashi* that hid his sex; his muscular torso gleamed with hard-earned sweat, and he shouldered an axe. A logger. She played her music, hummed along, acting as if she didn't know he was there.

He heard her tune, looked over and saw her. An expression of disbelief gripped his face, as if he'd seen a forest spirit. He wasn't skulking around in the bushes like one of the boys from town, come to gawk at her and lob stones at her shack. No. He pulled a handcart full of cut wood along the path to town; stopped and gazed; started walking, then stopped again.

She grinned. Her *Kimono* was tied loosely around her waist, and she knew he could see the ample curve of her breast, her long and shapely legs. She didn't meet his gaze, but she did lift her eyes in quick flashes, trying to gauge if she'd cast the proper spell.

At last he left his cart and walked around the lake to her, still holding his axe. And when he called out to her, his voice was as rugged as his physique, *"Konnichiwa."*

She dipped her head in reply, kept strumming the strings, not saying a word, trying to draw him closer. He kept his distance, however.

"You play beautifully," he said.

"*Domo*," she replied, breaking her silence. Perhaps her words would be even more attractive than her music. "I've not seen you before. Where are you from?"

He shrugged. "Many places. I am a *Ronin*, but with an axe for hire instead of a sword."

She gave a nervous little giggle, her eyes moving cautiously from her strings to the blade of his axe, then back again. "Are you in need of a place to stay?"

"I have a place, down in Chubu."

Masako's fingers froze. She felt the strong urge to get up and run inside. Had the townspeople hired his axe to chop more than wood?

"I'm Shingen," he told her. "What's your name?"

She looked up at him and frowned. "You say you've been to Chubu?"

He nodded.

"Then you've heard what they call me there?"

"Whore." There was no malice in Shingen's voice, and his eyes never left hers. "But that's not your name."

She glanced at her feet a moment, then her gaze rose to meet his once more. "Masako"

"Masako." Shingen's lips curled into a fetching grin. "A beautiful name for a beautiful woman."

She bowed her head slightly, her uneasy eyes drifting once again to his axe. "Do you really need that?"

"This?" He slid the handle off his shoulder, looked at her, sizing her up, then he studied his own reflection in the metal blade. "I suppose not."

When Shingen swung the axe, Masako could not help but flinch; he aimed at the ground, however, sheathed the blade in soft earth. She relaxed, but noticed that his fingers left the handle with more than a bit of hesitation.

"Did the townspeople send you here?" she asked.

He shook his head. "They warned me away."

"And yet still you came."

Shingen nodded; his eyes slid down the dark locks of her hair, over the black silk contours of her *Kimono*. "I wanted to see you for myself."

"And?"

"You're nothing like they described. You're stunning, the most amazing creature I've ever seen."

She could not help but smile at that. "Men don't go out of their way to visit an ugly whore."

It was Shingen's turn to frown. "So it's true then?"

Masako gave a single nod, but she did not shy away from his gaze.

They stood there for a time, studying one another, neither saying a word. They looked like statues, built to frame the white pillar of waterfall beyond. Finally, it was Shingen who spoke.

"What price would a poor logger have to pay for a kiss?"

"A kiss?" She grinned, taken aback. No man had asked her for a simple kiss before. "I think I can oblige you as a courtesy, to thank you for your kind words."

He approached slowly, as if trying to sneak up on a wild

animal, his eyes never leaving her face. When he reached her, he leaned in and pressed his mouth to hers. He did not use his tongue, nor did greedy hands try to grope her. His lips were rough and firm and heat radiated from his sun-kissed face.

She pressed back, tasting him, fear and adrenaline fueling her excitement, awakening something primal and instinctual. She broke away, her heart racing, afraid to take it any further.

"Domo arigato," Shingen whispered as he pulled back and stepped away.

"You're returning to Chubu?" she asked.

"Yes."

"I wouldn't mention this to anyone. It would make things difficult for you there."

He nodded, jerked his axe from the ground and shouldered it. As he walked to his cart, he glanced back at her more than once. *Did that really just happen?* the look said.

Masako wondered the same thing.

"And that's when you fell in love?" one of the children asked, lifting her eyes momentarily from her food.

"No, little one. We'd only just met." Masako had never believed in love, much less love at first sight. All she'd known from men was lust. There was something about this Shingen, however, something that told her he wasn't like any man she'd ever met. "And I liked him, and I could tell he liked me. That night, I actually dreamed about seeing him again."

"When *did* you see him again, Mama?"

She smiled. "The very next day."

———

He approached her shack with only a hint of reserve, a bright bouquet of flowers clutched in his hand. The axe, she noted, stayed back with his cart. "I saw these growing wild on the hillside and thought you might like them."

Masako stood in her doorway and offered him a nervous smile. *Flowers. Another first.* "They are most beautiful."

"Not nearly as beautiful as you."

She leaned over to accept Shingen's gift, her loose-fitting *Kimono* exposing much of her breasts. Masako saw his eyes linger, and her smile turned to a grin. She took the blossoms from his hand and lifted them to her nose; they smelled as wonderful as they looked. "*Domo.*"

Shingen's eyes rose to the roof, then slid down the walls of her shack. "It must get lonely out here, all by yourself."

"Yes," she agreed, running her fingers over soft, delicate petals. "How long do you plan to stay in Chubu?"

"Until the job is done. Perhaps longer, if I find more work." He glanced at his flowers in her hands, then turned to the waterfall. "This is gorgeous country."

"It is."

"Masako," he said, and it felt good to hear her name on his lips. "It pains me that there are superstitious men in this world, men who will never see the beauty of these woods. They sit in their homes, never leaving the towns where they were born, paralyzed by fear of what they have never seen, of what they do not understand and cannot—no, *will not* accept."

Her smile widened. "Would you like to come in?"

I want to, his eyes told her, but his frown said, *I shouldn't*.

"Just for some tea," she assured him. "To thank you for these lovely flowers."

Shingen nodded and followed her inside. He knelt down beside her hand-woven rug, his eyes sweeping the modest surroundings, then landing on Masako's bed roll. He turned away, watching her as she knelt to work at the stove. "Do you have enough wood for the winter? I can bring you some, if you'd like."

"Domo." She took the lid off her metal cooking pot. "It has been ages since I've made tea for someone else."

"Then I am honored."

Masako transferred steaming water into a deep bowl and carried it over. She knelt down, scooped powdered tea from her tea caddy into a shallow summer bowl, then poured hot water over it, whisking the mixture with great care. When it was just right, she held it out to him.

They exchanged bows, then Shingen took the bowl from her hands; he put it to his lips, and drank deeply.

"Wonderful," he told her, and from the tender look on his face, Masako thought he might be talking about more than just her tea.

She smiled and bowed again. "You are too kind."

They looked at each other in silence after that, and Masako could see heart and mind at war behind his eyes. She honestly didn't know which she wanted to win. He was a *good* man; he should have nothing to do with her, and yet she found herself aching for him.

At last, he set down his empty bowl and leaned in to kiss her. Masako's hands pressed on his brawny chest, not to push him away, but to feel the drumbeat of his heart. She slid her tongue past his rough lips and he met it with his own.

A spark ignited within her, the tingling warmth of desire; it spread like wildfire, threatening to engulf her whole. How many men had she lain with over the years? Dozens. And yet, she'd never felt this way with any of them. Perhaps—

No.

—with Shingen, it could be different. He cared for her, and she for him. If she were to lay with him—

No!

His hands were on her hips now, his grip firm and strong, but not demanding. She allowed him to pull her close and felt his erection rise, felt it pushing at the far-too-thin fabric of his *Mawashi.* She hated herself for wanting it, for wanting *him.*

A tear squeezed out from between her closed eyelids; now she did push him away, using all the strength she could muster, breaking the kiss before she passed the point of no return. She found herself out of breath, her heart still racing toward Shingen even as she pulled back. Somehow she managed words, "You should go."

Shingen blinked. "Why?"

"You *know* why. I'm a *Jorō—*"

"Yes, and it doesn't matter to me."

"But it *should.*" Masako tried to sound stern, but it was a poor attempt. "You deserve a future that isn't—"

"My future is with you."

She shook her head. What did he see in her? She was a pathetic creature, unworthy of such devotion. "Please..." She tightened the strap on her *Kimono.* "Please go."

Shingen nodded. He slowly got to his feet and moved to the door.

Masako wiped at her cheeks and called after him. "Don't come back. You need to find yourself a good woman, Shingen."

"I have."

She shook her head. "You don't want to fall in love with me."

"Too late," he told her, and then he stepped outside, leaving her to look after him with eyes that were as joyful as they were frightened.

That night, Shingen returned to Masako in her dreams and took her to bed. It felt so good, so *real.* But when she awoke, Masako found the hand between her legs was her own. Her fingers rubbed, slow and steady strokes, continuing the sensations her mind had begun.

This was yet another first. Sex had never been about pleasure before, at least not hers. But when she thought of Shingen...

Masako's fingers quickened their pace; they sunk deep inside her, sliding and stroking, pressure and friction awakening her every nerve. She moaned as the muscles of her arm tightened and stretched, her entire limb lengthening, becoming impossibly long and narrow, bending at sharp angles as new joints formed and flexed. A crop of coarse black hair sprouted from her skin, and her probing fingers were fused—flesh knitted together, nails honed to claws.

Masako screamed, her tingling pleasure killed by a sharp stab of pain; she withdrew her transformed limb, held it up before her eyes. Her claws glistened in the moonlight, covered in a slick of her own blood and fluids. She stared at them, sobbing.

"Please, Shingen," she cried, her lips trembling. "Please stay away."

————

"But he didn't stay away, did he Mama?"

Masako's eyes skimmed across the faces of her children like a pebble on the lake. "He tried. He tried very hard. Every day, he walked by this shack on his way back to town. And every day, he would look up and search for me. But he never left his cart.

"Sometimes, I would hide just inside the door, out of sight, and watch him pass. Other times, I would try to busy myself with chores, but even then, I could still feel him there."

A lump rose in her throat and she forced it back down. They had lived as mirrored reflections of loneliness and longing, every moment apart filled with memories of those passionate kisses and the fantasies of what might be possible if only they would allow it. But every action has a consequence, every road a toll that must be paid. Her children must know this.

"And finally," she told them, "he could not fight it anymore. And neither could I."

————

She'd been on her doorstep, playing her *Biwa*, gazing out across the lake. The tune was sad, like her mood. The water lay clear and placid; untroubled, uncomplicated, *pure*. How she envied it.

Shingen surprised her, emerging from the forest while the sun was still high in the afternoon sky. He was so tanned that his white *Mawashi* nearly glowed against his skin. He dropped his cart, loaded his arms with freshly cut wood, and approached her shack with a confident stride.

Masako stood, holding her instrument up as if it were a shield. "What are you doing?"

"I said I would bring you firewood for the winter. It will turn cold soon, and you should not be caught unprepared."

Looking at him now, she'd never felt so unprepared in her life. Nature gnawed at her bones; it clawed at the inner walls of her skin, begging to be unleashed. *Invite him inside, it said, lay with him, let him fill you with his seed, and be done with this torment.* She shook her head and gripped the neck of her *Biwa* until her knuckles turned white. "Just drop it there on the ground. I can bring it in later."

He paused. "You're afraid."

"Aren't you?"

"I would be, if I didn't love you."

Masako frowned. "You love *this*." She swept her body with her free hand. "*This* is not how I was born, Shingen. It's a deception, a *lie*."

"Then show me. Show me the real you."

"It does not work that way. I cannot control the change. It only happens—" She stopped herself.

He finished it for her, "When you make love."

"I've never made love," she confessed. "I've lain with many men, but there was never any love between us."

He stepped closer, and now she could smell him; a musky tang that made the blood boil in her veins. She pressed her thighs together, feeling the damp heat vent between them. *He needs to go*, she thought, *I don't know how much longer I can fight this.*

"I went to see the monk at a nearby temple," Shingen told her. "I asked him to remove this curse from you."

"This is not a curse, Shingen. It is who I am. It is *what* I am."

"The monk told me the same. He told me to forget you, to stay clear of this place, but how can I? Whatever you are, I love you."

"I'm the *Jorōgumo,* the binding lady, the monster they speak of in hushed voices, the evil whore that lives in the woods outside town."

"That's what people have called you, but that's not who you are." He dropped the wood on the ground, then walked right up to the edge of her step and looked her in the eyes. "I see no monster, no evil. I see someone who is all alone in this world, just as I am all alone. I see someone who can be stronger than she knows, someone with a beautiful heart, a beautiful soul...someone who I love, and who I hope loves me in return."

"I do love you." She blinked a tear from her eye. "And that's why, as much as I want you, we cannot *make* love."

"Masako—" He reached out, ran his finger down her cheek, and wiped her tear away. "—do not fear for me. I know what I want, what it means, but I cannot spend a lifetime wondering what it's like to be with you."

And then he kissed her, further weakening her resolve until it melted beneath the heat of her own passions. She loved him. She *needed* him. And when their lips finally parted, she offered no more objections.

With trembling fingers, Masako set her *Biwa* down in the corner of her shack, then worked the silken knot of her belt. The *Kimono* slid from her shoulders, dropped to form a black pool around her feet, and in her belly, she felt nightingales take flight; excitement or terror, she did not know which. Probably a good bit of both.

Shingen kissed her, embraced her, pressed his naked chest against hers. Masako felt the drumming of his heart; her own pulse like rolling thunder in her ears. She reached down blindly, fumbled with his *Mawashi*, her hungry lips never leaving his; she clawed, tore, and tugged at the thin fabric until it fell away in shreds. And then his manhood was in her hands; she stroked its swollen length, and felt the changes that had begun in her own flesh.

Masako's eyes snapped open; she broke the kiss and her gaze shot down, seeing a body that was familiar and alien at the same time. Her skin had darkened, blackened; bright yellow blotches appeared on her breasts and abdomen, coalescing into stripes and geometric shapes. Stray black hairs extended from her arms and legs; they brushed Shingen's skin, and she shuddered with pleasure at the sensation.

This is all happening too fast, she thought. With the other men, she had not changed until the sex was all but over, until the creature within called out for blood. She wondered what Shingen saw when he looked at her, what he thought of her now. *He'll be disgusted by the creature I'm becoming. The monster I* am. *He'll come to his senses, run away, and I'll never—*

Shingen touched her chin and lifted her eyes to meet his. "You're beautiful," he told her, then kissed her again.

Masako clasped his neck in her hands; she lifted her legs, wrapped them around his hips, and Shingen carried her across the room. He pressed her flat against the wall of the shack, and she felt every inch of him enter her. She grabbed a fistful of his hair and screamed for joy.

Four long, segmented legs burst into the world; one from each of Masako's shoulders, and one from either side of her abdomen just below her ribs; each was black with two wide, yellow stripes. Spider's legs. They enfolded Shingen, their clawed tips digging into his back and drawing blood. He grunted and clinched his teeth, but he did not halt his thrusts; if anything, they grew harder, faster, *deeper.*

We should stop this now, she thought, *while we still can, before it's too late*, but when her lips parted, she found the only sound she could muster was a short, high-pitched squeal. The sensations washed over her, one wave after another, with no time in between for her to catch her breath. Her eight limbs tightened around him, her groin grinding against his, her back sliding and arching on the wall; stiff, coarse hairs rasping across the wood, the vibrations nearly overpowering.

No, no, no...I can control it. I can be strong. I can, I can, I—

Then Shingen drove his full length deep inside her, as if to nail her to the wall, and Masako felt his seed explode into her in a single hot eruption.

Ohhhhh...

Masako's entire body stiffened and she threw her head back against the wall. Her eyes rolled, whites colored red, as if veins had burst and filled them with blood; they bulged from her skull, swelling to the size of small fruit, then birthing smaller red eyes that climbed her forehead and drifted back toward her shrinking ears. She screamed with pleasure, her jaw lengthening—the bone breaking in two, then spreading outward until her entire face split from the strain.

The head of a huge spider snapped forward, lunged for Shingen's throat. Mandibles clamped around his neck like a vice, fangs drilling deep into his arteries and filling him with venom. Before Masako even realized what she'd done, he convulsed and grew stiff in her embrace.

No, no, no, no...

She'd only lost control for a moment, an instant, but that had been all the creature inside her needed. She stared at Shingen's paralyzed form with her countless eyes, shaking her head, feeling numb. This was the fate to which he'd been so cavalier, the fate she'd hoped to spare him, but her primal nature would not be denied. She lowered him to the floor with great care, hating him for loving her, hating the feel of his heavy, dead weight in her arms.

Why wouldn't you listen to me? Why wouldn't you stay away? This was what you wanted? This?

Perhaps. Perhaps all the men who came to her door knew exactly what she was, what she would do to them, and found it a far more pleasurable alternative to days of poverty and hard living. Or perhaps they found death in the arms of a beautiful woman preferable to an unknown demise at a time not of their own choosing.

Masako shook her head. She could not know the minds of men. All she knew was that, in death, emperors and beggars all looked alike. And they all tasted just the same.

The creature grew restless, demanding to be fed.

I'm so sorry, my love. You were wrong. I'm weak. Forgive me.

She found herself hovering over Shingen, the craving that ruled her heart turning once more to blood lust. Her fangs dripped on her lover's bare chest. She watched the corrosive liquid eat through his skin, opening tiny holes that wept bloody tears.

Masako froze. Her entire body shook; unable to feed, unable to even cry. She lifted her head toward the ceiling, shook the wooden walls with a soul-wrenching yowl, then turned away.

She strutted out the door and down the steps as fast as her many-jointed legs would carry her. There was a breeze off the lake, and its coolness felt good against her sensitive hairs. Across the water, her countless eyes found Shingen's cart. Masako wanted the axe she knew he kept there, and as if on command, a thin silken rope shot from her body to retrieve it.

The tool whipped through the air on her line and swung at the ground; one side of its blade buried in the soft earth, the other side exposed and gleaming dangerously in the afternoon sun. Masako towered over it on her hind legs, ready to fall, to sheath the naked metal with her chest and cleave her aching heart in two. And then...

Movement.

In her abdomen, something fluttered and spun, fluttered and spun, again and again, the sensation multiplying until her belly began to visibly swell. Not her stomach, she realized. Her womb.

Masako backed away from the axe and slowly lowered all eight feet onto the cool grass. She ached to cry, but her spider's eyes still produced no tears. Children. Shingen's children.

Thank you, my love. Thank you.

She crawled back into the shack, back to Shingen. He remained a fallen statue on the floor, his arms outstretched in a hollow embrace she was meant to fill. The special glands at the rear of her abdomen were already feeding silk to her eager spinnerets.

There was much work ahead, and she hoped she had the strength to do it alone.

No, she realized, stroking her swollen womb, her hand already regaining its human shape, *Not alone. Not anymore.*

———

Masako finished her tale and lowered her eyes to the floor, to the food she'd laid out for her newborns. The body lay frozen in a rictus climax, bound in a cocoon of her making. Through the pale strands, she could still see dark eyes gazing up at her, not with accusations, but with understanding, with *love*.

"I wanted you to know something of the man who gave you life," she told their offspring. "I hope that one day...one day you will know true happiness, and when you do, I hope that you will be stronger than I was then, that you will be able to fight your instincts, that you will find a way to..."

Her voice trailed off with her thoughts and her vision blurred.

The impatient little *Jorōgumo* looked at one another, then turned their bulbous red eyes back to the shrouded form on the floor, their mandibles dripping. Finally one asked, "*Now* can we eat, Mama?"

Masako nodded and wiped away the tears. "Yes, children. Now you can eat."

HELL'S HOLLOW

Something bad was about to happen in Hell's Hollow. Sheriff Gleason felt it in his bones. He couldn't sleep, and when he finally crawled out of his bed, he found the street already choked with people, most of them strangers. The population of this little mining community had tripled overnight.

The sight of the town sheriff strutting down the sidewalk froze passersby in their tracks and killed their conversations, as if they were all keeping a secret from him, as if they were throwing some surprise party in his honor. Gleason hated surprises. He offered them a polite nod, a tip of his wide-brimmed hat toward the ladies, but he kept his hand on the butt of his revolver and his eyes alert.

A little skift of snow still clung to mountain tops, and a thick haze filled in the valleys, muting the early morning sun, but the trees and wildflowers made it obvious that spring was now in session. "How come a place that's so beautiful got a name like

'Hell's Hollow?'" That's what people asked as they passed through (nobody ever settled in the Hollow that didn't have business with the mine or the men who worked like moles down there in the dark coal). Well, the story goes that some wagons were passing by on their way out West when a man staggered up the old dirt road that leads down into the hollow, the road the town is still built around to this day. He was beaten within an inch of his life, and bleeding like a stuck pig. When the people in those wagons asked him where he'd been, he told them simply, "Hell," and that's been the Hollow's name ever since.

Gleason made his way through the crowds to the Boone Saloon. Lee Boone owned the place, tried to tell everyone that Daniel was his cousin. Some bought it, some didn't. Gleason landed firmly in the "didn't" column, but he never let on. The food and drinks were too damn good.

The place was packed, and so loud that a man couldn't hear himself think, much less listen to what anyone else had to say, but that changed as soon as Gleason stepped in. All eyes turned toward the door and a silence rippled through the crowd like wind through tall grass. The piano music went on for a minute or two after the conversations died—old Henry probably thought the patrons had finally shut up to hear him play for once. But then he too saw Gleason, and his smile faltered along with his fingers.

Gleason's eyes moved across the sea of faces, his hand still on his holster. He saw no immediate threat, however, so he made his way to the bar.

At least Lee Boone was still smiling.

"Mornin', Sheriff," Boone told him, his voice full of cheer.

"Mornin'."

"Your usual?"

Gleason nodded, keeping his eyes on the patrons. A few whispered to each other, but most sat speechless, still staring at him. "Quite a crowd," he said to Boone.

"Yes, sir."

"Some big to-do I don't know about?"

"Don't really know, Sheriff. But who am I to turn away payin' customers?"

Boone brought a plate loaded with biscuits and sausage gravy. He set it down on the bar in front of Gleason and started to turn away, but the sheriff reached out and grabbed hold of his wrist, pulled him closer. "What the hell is goin' on here, Lee?"

Gleason felt a tug on his pants leg. He looked down and saw a boy in overalls, no taller than his bar stool. The boy stared up at him with great curiosity.

"Sheriff," the boy said, "are you really a dead man?"

Before Gleason could answer, the boy's father rushed over. "Sorry, Sheriff. He don't mean nothin' by that, just repeatin' what he's heard."

"Who'd he hear it from?" Gleason asked, frowning. He turned back to Lee Boone, tightened his grip on the man's wrist.

Boone glared at the boy's father, then looked the sheriff dead in the eye. "Somebody's gunnin' for you."

"Who?" Gleason pressed.

"You wouldn't believe me if I told you."

"Goddammit, who?"

"Tolbert Johnson."

"Johnson?" Gleason's eyes narrowed and he struggled to calm himself. "I'm not in the mood for jokes, Boone!"

"It's no joke, Sheriff. Johnson came around last night, sayin' he was gonna find you and pay you back for sendin' those revenue boys out to his place."

"Boone, Tolbert Johnson's *dead*. Been dead and buried six feet down for a year now. I shot him myself."

The barkeep gave a slow nod. "You're tellin' the God's honest truth, Sheriff, but so am I. Johnson's dead, no denyin' that, but somehow he's up walkin' around again, and he's still gunnin' for you."

Gleason loosened his grip on Boone's wrist, and the man looked anxious to step away.

When President Rutherford B. Hayes took his seat up in that Oval Office, one of the first things he did was to start a crusade against moonshiners. He sent revenue agents climbing up and down every mountain in Appalachia looking for stills. Sure, when caught, most moonshiners just went to court, paid their taxes and their fines, and then went right back home, went right back to their stills and their shine, but not Tolbert Johnson. No. He gunned down the half a dozen agents that paid him a visit, then he came into town looking for more trouble. And trouble was just what he got.

A fly buzzed by the sheriff's ear and he waved it away. It landed in the gravy that topped his biscuits and rubbed its legs expectantly.

"I put a bullet right through his chest," Gleason said aloud to no one in particular. "He bled out in the street."

Boone nodded. "I know, Sheriff. I was there."

"Dead is dead. There ain't no comin' back from that."

Boone lifted his eyes to the door and frowned. "Try tellin' that to him."

"Gleason!"

The sheriff froze. His hand tightened on the butt of his revolver. His finger found the trigger.

That voice...it can't be!

But Gleason knew it was. He turned slowly, trying to steel his mind for the sight that awaited it, but there was no way to prepare for the impossible. What he saw standing in that doorway chilled him to his bones.

Boone was right. Tolbert Johnson was dead, there was no denying it. His face was now a bearded skull, the remaining flesh dry and splotched with black like burned parchment. His left eye was a vacant socket that reminded Gleason of the gaping entrance to the mine; the sheriff imagined things digging in there, busy maggots and beetles carrying out nuggets of brain matter instead of coal. Tattered clothes hung from emaciated arms and legs, and bullet holes pierced its shirt, like tiny windows to a shattered ribcage. And yet, somehow, the thing stood, the thing *spoke*.

"You sent them, didn't ya? They came askin' for folks runnin' shine, and you sent them right to my door, didn't ya?"

The same words, Gleason realized, the same anger, as if the raid had happened yesterday instead of over a year ago. Johnson knew the sheriff would be here having his breakfast, and just like the last time they'd met, he came ready for a fight.

Gleason's stunned eyes fell to the tarnished, rusty revolver the thing held in its boney hand. Would it have bullets? Would it even work after a year in the ground? He looked around at the crowd and decided not to take any chances.

"Johnson." The sheriff held up his gloved left hand, keeping his shooting hand ready to draw. "You've got nothin' against these people here. Let's take this outside."

The thing nodded. "Fine by me."

It backed out of the saloon and out of Gleason's sight.

"Whatcha gonna do, Sheriff?" Boone asked.

"Hell if I know, Lee. I haven't killed a lot of men in my time, and none of 'em twice." He drew a deep breath and made steps for the door. "Keep these people in here out of harm's way."

Boone nodded. "God be with you, Sheriff."

Gleason put his hand on the door, his mind moving a mile a minute. He'd put Tolbert Johnson down once. No reason to think he couldn't do it again.

'Cept Tolbert Johnson was a man. Flesh and blood from the mind o' God. This thing...this is some kinda witchcraft. This is the work o' the devil's hand. Who knows if a bullet can stop it? Who knows if it can be stopped at all?

"Gleason," the thing called, "don't make me come back in there after you!"

The sheriff pushed the door open and shuffled out into the street. Crowds lined the walkways on either side. In front of him, Johnson's corpse stood holding its rusty revolver; its single eye tracked Gleason's every move.

"I didn't wanna shoot them revenue boys," it yelled out. "But I had no choice. I gotta feed my kin."

Gleason eyed the rows of spectators. Some hoisted their children up on their shoulders to get a better look at the upcoming festivities. This is why they gathered. This was the show they'd all been waiting to see. Had there been this many a year ago, when he took the life from this man? Had it been such great sport to them then?

"Put down your gun, Johnson. We don't have to do this, not again. Go back to your grave where you belong!"

Confusion flashed in the dead thing's eye like lightning, there and then gone again. It grinned at him; its withered lips cracking and tearing like tissue paper. "Only one of us is goin' to their grave, Sheriff, and it ain't me. Now, draw!"

"Have it your way."

Gleason drew his revolver, his hand a blur. He fired. The bullet streaked down the dirt road, tearing a hole through the dead thing's tattered shirt and whatever remained of its chest beneath.

Johnson's eye widened. The corpse reached up, covered its wound with a boney hand. It teetered there a moment, then fired off a shot of its own before falling.

Gleason felt a sting in his chest and knew the thing's bullet had found its mark. He coughed and staggered up the street with his gun still drawn, waiting for the corpse to move again, waiting for it to try to stand. It did neither.

Johnson was dead again, hopefully for good this time.

The sheriff's strength left him. He dropped to his knees in the dirt next to Johnson's body, staring down at the remains, at the holes burned through its raggedy shirt. It only took one shot, just like the year before. A bullet through the chest, and Johnson had dropped like a marionette with its strings cut. But there were more than two holes there.

Many more.

Gleason reached out and laid his gloved hand on Johnson's bullet-riddled chest.

"R—rest now," the sheriff said, then slumped over and joined him in slumber.

———

The crowds clapped and cheered.

Inside the Boone Saloon, the boy in overalls looked up at his father. "They killed each other."

Boone laughed and smiled at him. "Yes siree, Bob. Always do. Just like clockwork. Same as the real deal back in 1881."

The little boy's eyes widened and he looked back out at the street, watching the volunteers pick up the bodies. "Where are they going?"

"They'll go back to sleep in their graves for another year. We bury them up right. Father Carole gives 'em Last Rites and everything." Boone chuckled. "Though, I don't know how 'last' it really is."

The boy's father patted his son's head and looked up at Boone. "Sorry my boy almost spoiled things."

"Don't worry about it. No harm done. I think we covered it up pretty well, don't you? Besides, I don't know how much they pay attention to the details. Hell, the sheriff still thinks I'm my grandfather every time. But we always have folks park their cars in the lot outside of town, just in case." Boone smiled back at the boy. "We wouldn't want the zombies getting' spooked, now would we?"

The boy nodded and his father asked, "So why does the sheriff remember the first shoot out?"

Boone shrugged. "He didn't used to. Who knows. Maybe he's like one of those lab rats you see in the newsreels. After doin' the same thing for so long, they tend to catch on eventually."

The man looked satisfied with that.

"So..." Boone rubbed his hands together. "You folks want to go ahead and buy your tickets for next year?"

"Not right now." The man picked his son up. "Maybe before we leave. Right now, I want to get my boy one of those big caramel apples and head over to that Showdown Hoedown they keep advertising."

"Well, make sure to tell all your friends what a good time you've had," Boone urged them. "Hell's Hollow: always one hell of a good time!"

INNER GODDESS

Elizabeth had never smelled an Egyptian mummy before. (Well, truth be told, she'd never smelled *any* mummy before.) They didn't have the same stench as the other long-dead-and-recently-exhumed corpses, the ones that came through her door for all manner of medical and chemical testing. Nor did they have the nice aroma of incense, of the various perfumes and oils used in the mummification process. Even the whiff of pine—from the resin that coated these linen strips and held them all together—had faded over time. Only a musty scent remained, like a box full of very old books.

Gone were the internal organs, the biggest contributors to the usual foul odor of decay. The priests had removed them all, placed them in ornate Canopic jars, then filled the empty body cavities with natron salt, with sawdust and flowers—drying them out, leaving no home for the stink of decomposition to take root. They'd done it carefully, reverently, with expert hands, and not just for the human bodies, either. They'd even done it for the cats.

So many cats.

They were the worst of it, the things that really gave Elizabeth the creeps. Those withered, vacant eye sockets... Those mouths full of teeth, frozen in rictus snarls... Some had a few stray whiskers extending like bits of straw from their emaciated snouts. And all had those perfectly-preserved little noses—black nostrils that stood out against wrinkled, brown skins.

She shuddered, her tongue suddenly sour and dry, as if these dehydrated creatures had sucked all the moisture right out of her mouth to—

What? Come back to life?

Elizabeth shook her head. Dead was dead. And she had seen enough death over the last four years to know that, whether it had been a few hours, days, months, or even centuries since these bodies had last tasted life, there was no power on this Earth that could revive them.

"Miss Wilson?"

At the sound of her name, Elizabeth blinked and looked up from the withered, smiling mummies all laid out in rows, reminded that there were other living people in the room. Professor Marsters stood on the opposite side of the table, staring back at her, acting as if everything was fine between them, as if nothing had happened.

Just another day at the office.

"Yes, Professor?" she replied. She'd never addressed him as anything other than "Professor," just as he'd never, in four years, used her first name. Not even during sex.

"I want you to begin taking samples of hair, bone, and soft tissue," Marsters told her, then his eyes swept the rest of their small group. "We'll be running the samples via radioimmunoassay and gas chromatography/mass spectrometry."

The others nodded, giving the professor their full, unquestioning attention, almost in awe of him. And why not? Marsters was a well-respected pathologist, one of the best in his field, and it was his association with Stanley University that convinced the Museum of Natural History to entrust them with these mummies for testing. Still, Elizabeth could not help but wonder what they would think of their mentor if they knew what he liked to do behind closed doors.

She rubbed her sore wrists. The marks the handcuffs had made lay hidden beneath her white scrub jacket and blue vinyl gloves, but she could still see them in her mind's eye. She could still feel the shackles biting her soft flesh and hard bone, as if she'd never really been freed.

"Will we be doing any DNA testing, Professor?" Adams asked. Elizabeth had done a lot of depraved things with Marsters, but it was *Adams* who had his nose up the man's ass.

"It would be pointless," Elizabeth told him. "The chemicals used in the mummification process preserve the mummies' appearance, but damage their DNA. Plus, we have nothing with which to compare it."

"Miss Wilson is quite right," the professor agreed. "While it might be possible to extract some minute amount of useable genetic information from the areas of these mummies least affected by any contamination, these are not the mummies of royalty."

He turned to look at one of the human mummies on the table behind him, a female, and gazed at the perfectly defined shape of its body, his gloved hand hovering over its tightly-wrapped chest. A look of great yearning reflected in his eyes. Elizabeth didn't know if anyone else could see it, but to her, it was painfully obvious.

She remained silent.

"They weren't given any sarcophagi of gold," Marsters went on to say, "nor were their names ever written on the walls of any tomb or monument. No, these are but a few of the hundreds of priests and priestesses of the Goddess Bast." He looked up at his students once more, his professional mask firmly back in place. "This, of course, explains why they were buried with all these cats."

Elizabeth's eyes drifted back down to the mummified animals. Finally, she understood. Bast had been the patron goddess of cats. Well, not *just* cats; she'd also been the goddess of women, and of secrets.

So many secrets.

Enough to fill those ornate, alabaster Canopic jars in the corner.

The affair alone would have been enough of a secret for Elizabeth to keep. After all, if anyone discovered that she'd been sleeping with her professor, it would have called into question all of her high marks and expert skills. As it stood now, with everything private, the professor's letter of recommendation would still hold weight. But it wasn't just the affair she had to keep secret; it was the aftermath of their "tutoring sessions" — all the bruises, the marks, the shame, and after last night...

She shuddered.

It started innocently enough, of course. It always did. The professor would suggest something, and Elizabeth would give a meek little nod and go along with it. That's how the neckties got introduced; smooth and silky, binding and yet not too uncomfortable. Then came the handcuffs; more restrictive, more *painful*. And then, last night...last night, he brought plastic wrap into the bedroom.

————

"When you die," Marsters began, kneeling down beside her on the bed, his eyes traveling the length of her naked body, "you will rot. All this lovely flesh will fall away, and, eventually, turn to dust. Nothing will be left of your beauty. Nothing will be left of you but your filthy bones."

He took the plastic wrap, the kind Elizabeth's mother used to preserve leftovers—

Oh, honey, if mother could only see you now! She warned you about these college professors, didn't she? Told you how they liked to take advantage of young, naïve co-eds like yourself? But did you listen? Nooooo. *You went right out and found yourself a professor with kinks your mother had never even dreamed of!*

—and he used it to lash her feet together, merge them into one bulbous mass. The wrap felt smooth against her skin, like the silken neckties he'd used in her initiation, but it was much lighter and far more constrictive.

"When the Egyptians died," Marsters went on to say, "they found a way to preserve the flesh, to make certain that every curve and contour of a beautiful female form would remain forever intact...forever desirable."

He slid his left arm under Elizabeth's knees and picked her legs up off the bed. As the thin plastic spiraled around her ankles and climbed up her calves, she marveled at its strength. She tried to flex her ankles, to move her feet apart, but found them almost completely immobilized.

"Are you worthy of forever, Miss Wilson?" Marsters asked, still wrapping, still *binding*; he was at her thighs now, her legs fused into one by the plastic.

"Yes, Professor," she replied, her voice trembling. The more these games escalated, the more painful and constrictive Elizabeth's shackles became, the more he seemed to enjoy it, and the more frightened she became of him.

But you keep coming back, don't you?

Yes, she did. No matter how much it hurt, no matter the shame she felt when it was over. All day long, she kept acting as if nothing had happened between them, and at night, she kept living in fear of what he might do to her if she ever told him "no."

Marsters reached the end of his roll, then went back over the lower half of her body with his hands, pressing and smoothing her wrappings until the plastic conformed perfectly to her shape. It was cool at first, but warmed quickly as it held onto her heat.

"Put your hands at your sides," the professor commanded, reaching for another roll.

Elizabeth did as she was told. She always did as she was told. *Pathetic.*

Marsters pulled her up off the bed, held her close to him as if to hug her. He was covered in sweat now, his work becoming more laborious with each round of wrapping. He bound her breasts, pushing them together, manipulating them to please his eye. And the entire time, Elizabeth saw that smile of his; the more corpse-like she became, the wider it grew.

She tried to move her arms, but they were now merged to her sides. Claustrophobia took hold of her, gripped her like a vice, squeezing every last drop of submission out of her and leaving nothing but white-hot fear in its place.

"Stop."

"Oh, but we can't quit now, Miss Wilson." His face remained bright with that wide, Cheshire Cat grin. "You're not finished."

Undaunted, the professor went on with his work. He wrapped the top of Elizabeth's shoulders, then moved to her neck. The plastic rounded her throat in tight circles like a noose.

"Stop," she cried again, terrified tears gathering in the corners of her eyes. "I mean it! Stop or I'll scream!"

But Marsters didn't stop. Instead, he quickened his pace, drawing the plastic up around her head and down under her chin, tightening it around her jaw like a muzzle to muffle her protests. The wrap refused to stick to her hair, but it clung tightly onto itself, and the professor kept circling her head with it, layer upon layer, until finally, he'd covered her over entirely.

Buried alive!

Paralyzed. Unable to squirm anymore, unable to twist, unable to arch her back, unable to even breath. All she could do was lie there, the smell of plastic thick in her nostrils. The tightly stretched wrap pressed down on her face until the bridge of her nose ached, and whenever she tried to draw breath, she deflated the small pocket of air over her eye sockets, snapping it taught against her wide, panicked eyes.

Marsters ran his hands over her entire body, smoothing the plastic down to accentuate her shape, her *curves*. She felt the pressure of his fingers through the wrap, the humid warmth radiating from her own body, the blood pulsing through her neck and temples, but all other sensations were muted.

Suffocating!

Her throat and chest were suddenly on fire.

Dying!

Through the translucent, plastic filter, the professor's face twisted and distorted into a devilish mask, but that crazed smile remained clear. Then, Elizabeth noticed something in his hand. Not a roll of plastic this time. No. This was something new, something *metal*; it gleamed in the lamplight like a—

A straight razor!

As she slipped into unconsciousness, Elizabeth tried hard to scream, but the resulting whimper was barely even audible outside the darkening plastic of her cocoon.

———

How long had she been out? A few minutes? An hour? Elizabeth had no idea. When she came to, she found herself free of the wrap, lying naked and shivering on sweat-soaked sheets.

"You're awake." Marsters brought her a glass of water, his tight, lunatic grin replaced with a slack expression of concern. "For a moment there, I thought we might have gone too far."

Elizabeth pushed herself back toward the headboard, then

pulled her legs up until her chin rested on her knees. He held the water out for her. She hesitated, then snatched the glass from his hand and drank deeply.

Marsters sat down on the edge of the bed. He reached over and ran his fingers through the wet tangles of her hair. Elizabeth cringed at his touch, but he seemed not to notice, or not to care. She thought it was more likely the latter.

"Sorry if I got a bit carried away, Miss Wilson," the professor told her, "but that was truly amazing. Thank you." He'd said it with the same matter-of-fact tone he might've used if she'd handed him a well-researched paper. "We have a busy day tomorrow, so I think I'll be off now. I'll see you bright and early in the lab."

Then, he gave her a pat on the head, as if to say she'd been a good dog. *Yes, an obedient dog. That's all I've ever been to him.* And with that, Marsters got up, gathered his things, and left her alone.

Elizabeth tried to set the empty water glass down on her bedside table, but her hands shook. The glass slipped from her grasp; it landed on her bedroom carpet with a thud, but it didn't break.

She pushed herself off the bed, her legs wobbling as she shuffled across the floor to the bathroom. The wastebasket was filled to the brim with wadded plastic wrap; Elizabeth kicked it over, and the first wave of sobs quaked through her.

———

Somehow, Elizabeth found enough strength to make it through the rest of the morning meeting. She stood there, with her arms crossed over her breasts, the memory of her own ordeal threatening to devour her from the inside with each passing moment, and she managed not to say a word about any of it. Her scholarships, her career, everything she'd worked so hard for all these years could all be thrown away like those wads of fucking plastic wrap.

And the bastard knows it. That's why he did it, why he picked me to do it to, because he knows I won't do a damn thing about it.

Elizabeth took a deep breath. The mummies' musk was preferable to the stench of sweaty plastic from the night before. She took her samples quickly, handed them off to Adams and others for their spectrum of tests, and when they left the room, she allowed herself to exhale.

"Time to check out the knickknacks," she said aloud, shifting her focus to a treasure trove of Egyptian artifacts in the corner. In addition to the canopic jars, there were other, far more priceless relics: golden statues, embalming tools, a few fierce-looking daggers, and all variety of jewelry; everything a goddess could want.

One piece in particular caught her attention: a beaded necklace. She picked it up, the stark light from the overhead lamps illuminating its striking colors—beautiful shades of yellow and red—reminding her of the cat's eye marbles she'd played with as a child.

Appropriate for the goddess of cats.

Dangling from the center, giving the necklace weight, was a

golden disk etched with hieroglyphs—curved lines around an open eye. The pupil seemed elongated, almost elliptical.

"Put it on."

The voice echoed through Elizabeth's brain like a gunshot. She flinched and turned her head, wondering which of her peers had made the suggestion, but there was no one else in the room. At least, no one living.

Nobody here but us mummies.

Elizabeth frowned. Her gaze returned to the golden disk in her hands, to the pictographs. There was no denying the craftsmanship. It looked and felt...*regal.*

And then, Elizabeth saw herself wearing it. She stroked her neck and ran her fingers down to the edge of her V-neck collar, imagining what it would be like. The beads, the gold, they were as beautiful now as the day they were forged. She studied the hieroglyphs, curious of their meaning.

I shouldn't do this, she thought. *If someone sees me...*

"No one is watching." The stranger's voice again, and this time she knew that it was only in her head. *"No one will see.*

"Put it on."

Elizabeth paused. She lowered her hand a bit, ready to set the necklace back on the table where it belonged, then she looked around the room again. The voice was right. No one would see her. No one would say a thing.

Can't say a thing, remember. Can't ruin your life.

What harm would there be in trying this on? No harm at all. None.

"So, put it on."

Elizabeth lifted the necklace up over her head and let it rest on her shoulders. She adjusted it, moving the heavy disk so that it covered her heart. And once it was on, Elizabeth felt strangely different; she stood erect, her chin held high.

"It suits you." The voice again, but this time it was no longer confined to her skull. It came from behind her.

Elizabeth spun around.

A beautiful, half-naked woman stood in the opposite corner of the room. Blue straps crisscrossed between her bare breasts, holding up a skin-tight red garment that clung to her, covering her stomach, hips and legs. There were gold details in the fabric —stripes, bands and scales, and along the hem, a strip of hieroglyphs.

Jeweled rings adorned the woman's fingers, and her forearms were embraced by a dozen or more golden hoops. Around her biceps, she wore thicker manacles, gold with a strip of blue through the center. A long beaded headdress —again, blue with bands of gold—cascaded down her back and flowed over her shoulders. And poking up through the beads on either side of her head were large, triangular ears.

Cat's ears.

The woman's entire face was that of a cat. At first, Elizabeth thought it was only make-up, a face-painting design she'd seen at countless carnivals, but when she blinked and looked closer, Elizabeth knew the fur was real. It was short, beige all over, but white around the woman's mouth; black "tear marks" ran from the corners of her high-set, slanted eyes down the sides of her nose to a pair of glossy black lips. And when those lips parted, Elizabeth heard a sultry, breathy voice punctuated by purrs.

"Are you content, child?" the woman asked, then shook her

feline head. *"No. You are not content at all. How can you be, when you are a slave?"*

At the sound of her voice, every mummified cat on the table began to stir. Their long, withered tails swished through the air and they rolled over onto bandaged legs. Their leathery faces turned toward her, every vacant socket in their tiny skulls focused on her piercing eyes. She reached down to pet them, running her long, dainty fingers across their arched, emaciated spines.

"It is easy to see why the dog is man's *best friend, while we prefer the company of cats."*

She looked up, stared directly into Elizabeth's eyes, and Elizabeth pressed herself against the lip of the table, her breath caught in her throat.

"Dogs are obedient," the cat-woman went on to say, *"submissive. They do what their masters tell them to do, and they do it without question. The masters order; they obey."*

Her gaze returned to the mummified creatures swarming around her, clawing at each other for a turn in line, each longing for her touch.

"But cats," she said, *"cats have a mind of their own. Trying to order a cat about is like trying to tell the sun not to rise, or the wind to blow in a different direction. Cats yield to no one. They have no master."*

The cat headed-woman glided across the room, her stride as smooth and silky as the garment she wore.

"Do you know who I am, Elizabeth?"

My name, Elizabeth thought. *This* thing *knows my name. How does it know my name?*

"Come now, girl, you summoned me. Surely you can speak my name?"

And, of course, Elizabeth *did* know her name. She'd known almost immediately, but she hadn't been able to believe it. She *still* didn't believe it. "Bast?"

"Yes, child." The goddess nodded, her black lips curling into a pleasant grin. She moved away from the tables, closer to Elizabeth.

One of the dead cats turned and leapt onto the floor to follow, but on impact, its brittle forelegs snapped off in a cloud of dust.

"You are such a beautiful girl, Elizabeth. More beautiful than you know. More powerful *than you know."*

Elizabeth shook her head, denying it, denying everything. She was still at home, still curled up in her sweaty sheets, with the stench of plastic in her nose and tears crusting in the corners of her eyes.

"*I am a* goddess," Bast announced, her sultry voice changing, deepening until it boomed like thunder. *"If I say you are power-ful, then it is so."*

"Fine!" Elizabeth winced. She cringed back against the table, gripping the edge until her knuckles turned white. "I'm powerful. I'm Wonder Woman. Just, please... I... I haven't done anything wrong."

"No," Bast agreed, *"but you have* been wronged." The goddess grew closer still, and now Elizabeth could smell her perfume; an intoxicating cocktail of lily, henna, and cinnamon. *"Yes. I can see it in your eyes, child: your whole sad, sordid history...a life full of pain, full of self-loathing and anxiety, so*

much anxiety. You really are frightened of your own shadow, are you not?"

Elizabeth said nothing. She frowned and turned away, watching the re-animated cats as they lined the edge of the other tables. Their shriveled, bandaged tails fanned the air; their naked fangs glowed in the lamplight.

"Look at me!" Bast roared.

Elizabeth looked up with a start. The goddess now towered over her, staring down at her with the bright, predatory eyes of a lioness.

"I have helped many others like you over the centuries," Bast told her. *"Countless poor souls, slaves to their own fear, the weak and the wounded, I have set them free."*

The goddess combed Elizabeth's hair with her ringed fingers.

"I can help you, too, child. If you desire it, I can give you the self-confidence you lack. I can give you the power you need."

Elizabeth's scalp tingled at Bast's touch. Her hair came alive, twisting and snaking around the goddess' hand; dead cells brought to life anew. Just like the cats.

"All you have to do is ask." Bast moved her hand down Elizabeth's cheek; tingling warmth radiated from her fingers, invigorating Elizabeth's entire body. *"You do want it, don't you, child?"*

"Yes," Elizabeth heard herself saying. She closed her eyes, enraptured by the goddess' touch, by the sweet smell of her perfume, by the soothing sound of her purr, and most of all, by all her promises. "I'm tired of being *afraid.* I want it! I want it more than I've ever wanted anything! Please...give it to me!"

"Miss Wilson!"

Elizabeth's eyes sprang open. Bast was gone, and in her place stood Professor Marsters. The legless, mummified cat now laid motionless on the tiled floor at his feet.

He looked up at her, at the beaded necklace she still wore, unable to hide his anger. "What the hell is going on in here?"

Elizabeth took off the necklace and set it back on the table, smoothing her hair with her hand. "I was just..."

"May I have a word with you in my office?"

Elizabeth knew it was an order, not a request. And like a faithful dog, she obeyed.

———

When the door closed, Marsters wasted no time in cutting to the chase. "I'm recommending Mr. Adams for the Shelby Labs position."

Elizabeth felt as if she'd just been punched in the stomach. "You're what?"

"It's simple, really, Miss Wilson. You've both applied for the same position, and I feel he is the more qualified candidate."

"*Adams?*" Her eyes narrowed. "And what did you do with *him* in the bedroom?"

He flashed a disappointed glare. "Mr. Adams' work in the lab is exemplary. And, after what I just witnessed—"

"You unbelievable bastard."

Marsters frowned. "Miss Wilson, really, I—"

"I'll call the police."

"Because I didn't recommend you for a job?"

"Because you *raped me!*"

Marsters chuckled at that.

"He laughs *at you, at your* pain." Bast's voice again, ringing through Elizabeth's head. *"He believes you are weak, a dog that can be ordered about. Show him that he is sorely mistaken, that you are* strong."

"Don't think I won't do it," Elizabeth warned. "I'll tell them what you did to me. The cops, the university... I'll ruin your whole career!"

Marsters didn't even blink. "And I'll tell them that you are a spurned ex-lover, and a distraught one at that—a woman who made such an accusation only *after* I recommended someone else for a position she wanted."

And then it hit her. "You *planned* this."

"You give me far too much credit—"

"And *you* left the plastic wrap in my trash!"

"Yes," Bast urged. *"Do not let him win. You have the power. You are a* lioness!"

Elizabeth leaned across the desk, her eyes narrow, her voice strong, stronger than it had ever been in her life. "I'm sure the wrap will have your fingerprints on it. They'll believe me then. They'll—"

"They'll realize that we had a long-standing, *consensual* relationship. Nothing more." The professor produced his iPhone and slid it across the desk to her. "After all, Miss Wilson, if a picture says a thousand words, what sort of story will a thousand pictures tell?"

She reached over and picked up his phone. There, displayed on the screen, was a photo of Elizabeth, naked, blindfolded, handcuffed to the headboard, and worst of all, smiling. The date in the lower right hand corner told her it had been taken over a year ago.

"Does that look like a woman who was raped?" Marsters asked.

No, it looks like a scared little girl.

"There are many others," he told her with a smile. "You have to love cell phone cameras. With no flash, not even a sound, they take such quality photos. Go ahead, thumb through them."

Elizabeth did just that, finding picture after picture of herself in one compromising position after another. The dates were all different, as were the rooms—her bedroom, his bedroom, the hotel room at a seminar in Baltimore last fall—but the overall impression was the same. Here was a woman who wanted it, wanted *him.*

Her first thought was to erase the entire folder, but Marsters knew that. He seemed to know everything.

"Those aren't the only copies, of course. I have a duplicate file saved in a safe place, a place where no one would ever need to see them...unless, of course, they are needed in my defense."

Hot bile rose in Elizabeth's throat, and when she forced it down again, she nearly choked. The office walls were closing in. She felt smothered, trapped.

If he ever showed these to anyone...I'd die.

"Do not give him a chance," Bast told her mind's ear. *"Do not let him hurt you again. Not you. Not anyone."*

"Now, my dear Miss Wilson," Marsters reached up and took the phone from her trembling hand, "the best thing for you to do is to go back to the lab, clean up your little mess, and never breathe a word of this to anyone."

He leaned back in his chair, his smile widening. Oh, how Elizabeth wanted to rip that smile from his face. How she wished she could do that and more to him.

"If you can manage that," the professor went on to say, "you may yet get a passing grade for the semester. Have I made myself clear?"

"Very clear." Elizabeth backed away from the desk, anxious to put distance between her and Marsters. She hurried down the hall to the lab, to Bast.

———

The hallways were dark and deserted. Had someone else been there, they might have seen Professor Marsters slip from his office, might have watched as he locked the door behind him and started for his car. They might have noticed the briefcase he held in his hands, might have heard the jangle of his keys. But there was no one else to see or hear anything.

Only Elizabeth.

She stepped from the shadows, her hands in the pockets of her lab coat, the Egyptian necklace back around her neck where it belonged. "Professor?"

Marsters turned. "Miss Wilson...what are you still doing here?"

Elizabeth offered him a sly little grin in reply. "Chatting with our guests."

"Guests?"

"The mummies, silly." Her grin widened. "The priests and priestesses of Bast."

Marsters frowned and rolled his eyes, but he didn't back away from her, and he didn't run. Why should he? He was the master, after all, and she was his meek, *obedient* little dog.

"They've taught me quite a bit about the whole mummification process." She took another step toward him. "I'm sure you'd find it fascinating."

"Really, Miss Wilson, I don't—"

"Are you worthy of forever, Professor?"

Before he could say another word, she removed the taser from her pocket and shoved it into his crotch.

———

After what seemed like an eternity to Elizabeth, Marsters' eyes finally fluttered open.

"You're awake." She tightened the last of the restraints that held him to the gurney, then wiped the sweat from her forehead. "For a moment there, I thought we might have gotten carried away."

She held up her taser.

"75,000 volts. A high school graduation present from my mother. She was so *worried* I would run into some sicko here on campus. Boy, was she right!"

Elizabeth chuckled. And when she reached over to brush the hair from his face, he recoiled from her touch. She couldn't help but smile at that.

Marsters lifted his head to look at his bonds, then glanced around the room, his eyes widening. All around him, the mummified cats gathered, crouching at the edge of the tables with their tails swishing and their fangs bared. The priests and priestesses of Bast were there as well, standing at the ends of the gurney, smiling their eternal grins. Elizabeth couldn't help but wonder what he thought of their tightly wrapped bodies now.

"You know," she began, turning away, "I should really thank you. Before last night, I was this sad, pitiful little thing who would never have stood up for herself in a million years. Then you abused—no, you *tortured* me, suffocated and buried me in plastic, and I was re-born."

She walked over to the relic table, found one of the ceremonial daggers, and snatched it up.

"Now, we have a busy night ahead of us, Professor, so I think we should get started."

"Please, Miss Wilson... Elizabeth..."

"Wow!" She spun to look back at him. "You actually know my name!"

"Think about what you're doing."

"Oh, believe me, *Professor*, I have." She held up the dagger, admiring the seated cat that formed its golden hilt. "I've done nothing all day but think about it."

"Please." He squirmed on the gurney, tried to pull free of the restraints. "Please...stop."

"But you're not finished." She pointed at him with the blade. "How many innocent girls have you hurt over the years? How many did you rape before me?"

"I'm sorry," he said. "Truly, I am. But—"

"I'm sorry too," she told him, but not believing a word of it. She wasn't as naïve as she'd been the day before. Not by a long shot. And it was all due to *her*. "I'm sorry those other girls didn't have Bast to help them."

The goddess stepped from the shadows, her beaded headdress flowing over her shoulders and down her back. *"Content, my child?"*

Elizabeth bowed her head. "Very, my goddess."

Marsters seemed to take no notice of Bast. No. His terrified eyes were focused squarely on Elizabeth, on the blade she held in her hand.

"She's not only the protector of cats, you know." Elizabeth walked back to the gurney, waving the dagger as if conducting a symphony. "She's also the goddess of women."

"And of secrets," Bast purred, following her.

"She wanted me to cut out your tongue," Elizabeth smiled, "so you wouldn't be able to tell anyone what we'd done, your version of it anyway. So you wouldn't be able ruin my life."

"You're insane," Marsters said, and then he cried out for help, screamed at the top of his lungs.

Elizabeth pulled off his necktie and gagged him with it. "I told her that wasn't good enough. You see, if I cut out your tongue, you'd still be able to hurt other women."

She took the blade and moved it slowly down his body to his crotch. Tears formed watery veins down his cheeks and he moaned into the tie.

"But, that's still not the root of the problem, is it? No, your sickness is in your head." Elizabeth pointed at her own temple with the blade. "In your *mind*."

She walked back over to the relics. The mummies followed her with their desiccated eyes, knowing what was coming, what they had prepared her for. Their leathery lips pulled back to reveal even more of their teeth.

Bast leaned back against the opposite table, petting her beloved cats. *"Tell him what you want, child."*

Elizabeth smiled. "I want to play your game again, Professor. Just one, little difference..."

She selected something else from the table: a long, golden rod with a hook on the end; an Egyptian embalming tool, used to remove the brain through the nose prior to wrapping. She held it up for Marsters' inspection.

"Tonight, it's your turn to be the mummy."

UNKOWN CALLER

B rian still wore black. He'd worn black for one year, four months, six days, and eighteen hours. And every now and then, some well-meaning, annoying friend or co-worker would approach him, would lightly touch his arm, place a comforting hand on his shoulder, or worst of all, take his hand in theirs, all with that horrible look of pity in their eyes. They would tell him how sorry they were, and then they would go on to inform him of some tired banality, as if they were the first to have ever mentioned it.

"At least she didn't suffer."

"You can't live in the past."

"Life goes on."

They were all right, of course. Life *did* go on. And on. And on. No matter how much he wished it would just simply end and be done with him.

Each night, he would close his eyes and find her waiting for him there in the dark, naked on the bed they shared. He could smell her sweet perfume, run his fingers through her hair. And when he looked deep into her eyes, he saw his own longing mirrored there. But each morning, when the sun crept through the slats in his blinds, painting hot stripes across his room, he had to open his eyes once more, had to see that he was alone, had to deal with the fact that she was gone.

But life goes on. Each new day following another, footprints in the sands of time. Every stride carrying him further and further away from her. And he could do nothing to stop the march.

No. He moved through the world with numb detachment, in a perpetual state of shock, his mind still reaching out for her, watching helpless as she slipped from his grasp, growing more and more distant, her features gradually becoming hazy, indistinct. He tried to recall the music of her voice, and the tune escaped him. Oh, the words were still there, but the melody was off, and no matter how hard he tried, he could not make it sound right to his inner ear.

Brian went to Chapel Hill Cemetery, walked up to her grave. He stood in somber silence, staring at her name etched in granite, and he fought the impulse to scream, to beat the stone with his fists until his hands were bloody pulps, all the while watering her flowers with his tears. The urge soon passed, however. The blooms would dry and wilt, just like the ones before them, and the ones before those; endless repetition.

Life goes on. The world kept turning like a Tilt-a-Whirl left unattended. And the operator just sat back and let it spin, oblivious to the fact that one of its passengers had fallen off the wheel.

"Anita?" Brian said aloud. "Where did you go? You were here, and we were happy, and now..."

Now she was gone, and there was just this cold stone to prove that she'd ever been here at all; and in his chest, a smaller, colder replica marked the spot where his heart had been. And the dates of death on both markers were exactly the same.

And all around them, life went on. The wind blew. The rain turned to snow and then back into rain. The first anniversary of their love came and went and now came again. God couldn't even give them a year together. Not even a single year.

It wasn't fair.

No. It wasn't fair at all. But there was nothing he could do to change it. Anita would always be here...asleep beneath his feet in the cold, uncaring ground. And he had to let her rest, didn't he? Yes. He had to let go of the dead and move on with the living, no matter how miserable he might be. It was expected of him. Society demanded it.

"You can't live in the past."

"Life goes on."

"Goodbye, my love." Brian reached out and touched the stone, smooth face yielding far too quickly to a rough, craggy edge. "Goodbye."

He started to turn away when his cell phone rang; a tune he hadn't heard in ages. James Blunt's "Beautiful." Anita's ringtone.

Brian reached for it, stared at the display, half-expecting to see his wife's smiling face, the way it had appeared whenever she'd called him during the day. Anita loved her phone almost as much as she loved him. It was constantly in her hand, as if it were a part of her. Facebook. Texts. Calling him every few hours to tell him how much she missed him and couldn't wait for him to get home. So, when the memorials ended and it came time for her to be buried, he'd placed her beloved phone in her cold, dead hands, wishing it could be him in the coffin with her instead.

His screen was black, however. No name. No number. Just the words "Unknown Caller" in glowing white letters. But before Brian could answer, the tune ended. The lighted screen went dark, filled with the reflection of his own haggard face, and he continued to stare down at it with stupefied eyes.

If he'd been quicker, would he have heard Anita's sunny voice?

"Hey there, handsome! Just called to say I love you."

Would he have known it instantly, or would it have been a struggle to place it?

"Hurry home. I'm waiting for you."

He looked up at the sky. It was light blue, cloudless, reminding him of Anita's eyes. He pinched his own eyes closed, kneaded the lids with his thumb and forefinger. For his own sanity, he had to stop thinking of her, had to—

The cellphone vibrated in his hand.

Brian's eyes sprang open and he saw the tiny icon of an envelope on his screen. A new text. Probably a friend or co-worker, an invitation to some event or get-together, designed to pull him from his melancholy. He opened it, anxious for any distraction, not believing what he found.

MISS YOU <3

Again, no name, no number, but he knew the sender by the

little heart signature she always used. It was a message he'd received countless times in the past, one that had always brought a smile to his face, no matter how his day had been. In fact, he felt one dawning now.

Brian shook his head, a sudden gust of September chill making him shudder. It couldn't be Anita. *Couldn't be.* Anita was gone. He glanced back down at her tombstone, the monument to their sundered love, as if in need of confirmation.

"Anita?" he whispered, then covered his mouth with his hands, as though he were shocked by the sound of her name spoken aloud.

No, no, no...The very idea...*too outlandish, too dangerously unbalanced to even consider...*

And yet he stood there, six feet over her, cell phone in one trembling hand, considering it. He wondered how long a battery would last down there, in the dark, in the dampness, then he wondered if she were really down there at all. Maybe the doctors had made a mistake? Maybe—

Maybe I'm losing my mind?

Brian backed away from her grave, from the edge of madness, then turned and hurried off to his car. He felt calmer with each step, more rational. Someone had the wrong number. That was all. And, when Brian didn't answer the phone to inform them of their error, they just sent a text to that same wrong number. Simple as that.

But it was the same text that—

—that thousands of people probably send to their loved ones each and every day.

Brian nodded, wondering why the certainty of reason

saddened him further. He drove home in a daze, tossed his clothes on the floor with absentminded familiarity, then climbed into the shower. He closed his eyes and turned his face up toward the showerhead, his tears lost to the dousing spray.

As he stood there, warm water fighting off the cold he felt in his bones, in his *soul*, he became aware that he was no longer alone. Someone was there in the shower with him, standing right behind him. Before Brian could open his eyes, he felt hands sweep up his face to cover them; soft hands, with long, delicate fingers.

"Guess who," said a beautiful, nearly forgotten feminine voice, "and you better get it right the first try."

"Anita?"

She giggled. "Bingo!"

He spun around to face her, his eyes wide with shock and relief, with fear and joy, with—

"Hey, it's okay." She smiled, her teeth like strings of pearls, her skin like alabaster. "I didn't mean to startle you, sweetie. Just thought you might like some company."

"But...you can't be here." Brian ran his trembling fingers through her long, dark hair, his unbelieving eyes still locked with hers. "You're...you're dead."

She giggled again. "Dead?"

He nodded in her hands; her soft, beautiful hands.

"Don't be silly, babe," she told him, still smiling. "Could a dead woman do this?"

And then she kissed him. Her lips were succulent, soft and warm. Her breasts, pressed against his chest, were as supple as he remembered them. And her tongue courted his in the comfortable, intimate dance they'd shared so many times before. It was her. Somehow, she was back in his arms again.

"God," Brian said as they parted, his throat tightening, his tears turning from despair to elation. "I just had the most horrible nightmare. You died and I—"

She pressed a finger to his lips to silence him. "Let's not talk about something so horrible. I can think of something much more pleasant to be doing right now. Can't you?"

And then she kissed him again and again, pressing her body against his, wanting him, needing him as much as he needed her. He stirred to arousal and pushed her back against the wall. She breathed into him as her arched back slid up the wet tile; her legs rose up, wrapped around his hips, enveloped him. Brian drove himself deep inside of her; her sweet moans filled his ears, echoing through his brain like a distant memory.

Because that's all this is. The ghost of intimacy. A dream of lost communion, gone now forever.

No. No, she was here with him. She was *real*. And he could feel her fingers grip his back, feel the rhythm of her heart beneath her heaving breasts, feel her lips against his ear, telling him how much she loved him, how much she *ached* for him. He could hear the words, over and over, like a recording stuck on repeat.

*Her voice...it sounds odd...*wrong.

Because it is *wrong, my friend. You can't live in the past. Life goes on.*

NO! Brian closed his eyes and clinched his teeth. He held Anita tightly to him, and his thrusts grew deeper, more rapid, almost angry in their intensity.

Her moans rose in pitch, blossoming into screams, not of ecstasy, but of anguish, of misery. And suddenly Brian realized it wasn't Anita screaming at all. The screams were his own, screams at the injustice of it all, screams for a life that could have been and wasn't.

———

When Brian finally opened his eyes once more, he found himself naked on his side of the bed. His side. That was a cruel joke. The whole fucking bed was his now, wasn't it? And it felt just as vast and as desolate as a desert.

He swallowed, wincing at the burning pain in his throat. And when he tried to move, he found that his muscles ached as if they'd been clenched for far too long.

Something vibrated in his hand, startling him.

His cell phone.

Brian held it up to his face, wiped the grit of stale tears from his eyes, and tried to focus on the screen.

YOU HAVE 1 MISSED CALL.

YOU HAVE 1 NEW MESSAGE.

With a swipe of his thumb, he checked his call log for the number, found only the words "Unknown Caller" and moved on to voicemail. Empty. He did find a text, however; three innocent words that blew a draft of horror down his spine.

HEY THERE, HANDSOME. <3

Anita's words.

Anita's little heart signature.

Brian's hand shot to her side of the bed, felt for the slightest hint of warmth, some sign that their coupling had been something other than his own desperate fantasy, desperately wanting her death to have been the nightmare, but the sheets were ice cold. Her pillow held only the ghost of her fragrance.

She truly was gone.

Of course she was. Brian still had all the covers. Anita was always cold, and would steal them from him so that he would wake up shivering. He'd always hated that. Now he'd give anything to be cold in the night.

He missed everything about her, especially those texts with the stupid little hearts.

But these messages couldn't be from her. He knew that. Brian had kissed her forehead and slid her cell phone between her frigid fingers. He'd watched them close the coffin lid on her, saw them latch it—the same coffin he'd seen resting on those chrome runners, suspended above that bottomless pit of an open grave.

But I never saw them lower her down, did I? he recalled, grasping for some glimmer of hope. *I never saw them cover her over with earth, never—*

Stop living in a fantasy! reason shouted back. *She's dead. That's the reality of it, and you damn well know it!*

Then if not her, who? Who's calling with her *ringtone? Who keeps sending me texts in* her *words?* Who? *And* why?

His phone sat mute, offering no answers.

Brian turned it over and over in his trembling hand, working up the nerve to call the number back. Finally, he hit the button, listened to the ringing in his ear, afraid of what he would hear when the other party answered, afraid some ghostly voice might actually speak his name.

Instead, an automated answering system came on the line. "The caller you are trying to reach...is not available. At the tone, please record your message."

Beep.

"Uh...Hello," Brian stammered, trying to think of what to say when he didn't know who would hear it. "I—I got some calls and texts from this number. I think you're trying to reach someone else." He ran his fingers through his still-damp hair. "If you call back and I don't pick up in time, please leave me a voice message with your name and the reason for your call. Thanks."

He disconnected the call and slowly dropped the phone from his ear, staring at the darkened screen, feeling anxious and stupid.

———

The cellular store clerk wore glasses with trendy frames and a corporate smile that bled into her voice. "Hi, I'm Heidi. How can I help you today?"

"I need to know where some calls and texts are coming from." Brian held up his phone. "Is there a way to find out who's dialing from an 'unknown' number?"

"Hmmmm..." Heidi's smile turned to faux curiosity. She tilted her head to look at his missed call display, then asked, "Have you tried calling it back?"

"Of course I've tried calling it," he snapped. "I just get an automated voice mail. It doesn't even tell me whose mailbox it is."

"I see," she said respectively, then offered up another cheery suggestion. "Did you try Googling the number to see what comes up?"

"I don't *have* a number." He tapped the screen with his fore-finger. "See? Unknown."

She nodded, bemused. "Well, when someone goes to the trouble of blocking their identity, they're usually up to no good. If they're harassing you, I can show you how to use the settings on your phone to block—"

"No," Brian barked at her, then fought to keep his voice level, "I don't want to *block* the calls. I need to know who's making them."

No, you need to know if it's your wife—your dead wife. Isn't that what you really *need to know?*

"Can I take a closer look at your phone?" Heidi asked.

Brian shrugged and handed it over to her.

The clerk knew her way around his phone better than he did. Using both thumbs, she accessed his logs and settings, pausing a few moments to read one bit of information before moving on to the next.

"It's probably another cell phone," she told him. More thumbing. More reading. "I'm trying to see if you're equipped with the Star 57 feature."

"Star 57?"

"It's the Appropriate Call Trace Code. If you have it, you can dial *57 while you're still in the middle of the call, or immedi-ately after the call ends, and after three calls from the same number, the police get notification of the harassment." She frowned and handed back his phone. "But it looks like this model isn't equipped with that feature."

"So what do you recommend?"

Heidi beamed. "We could upgrade you to a new phone that has the feature."

A sales pitch. Of course. He should have known.

"No thank you," Brian grunted. "Anything else?"

She shrugged. "There's some tracer software you can get online, but I wouldn't recommend you download it. You never know what you're getting, and most of it will just screw up your phone." She shuddered for emphasis, then added, "You might have to hire a private investigator."

Or you could just go back to Anita's grave, his mind offered, half-jokingly. *Call the number back while you're standing there, see if her phone rings. If nothing happens, you can drop this insanity once and for all and finally move on with your life. You can't live in the past, remember?*

"Is there anything else I can help you with, sir?" Heidi asked. The smile was gone from her voice now. He wasn't buying, and she was clearly anxious to move on.

"Yeah," Brian said thinly. "You can tell me if a ringtone can be heard through a coffin and six feet of dirt."

Heidi gaped at him, dumbfounded.

———

He stopped by the grocery store to purchase flowers, even though he'd just left Anita a fresh bouquet the day before.

Approaching her grave without flowers seemed wrong somehow. She loved flowers almost as much as she loved her cell phone, which was almost as much as she loved him.

Brian's heart thudded heavily in his chest. And in his mind, he wondered what he would do if he actually heard a ring.

It's not going to happen, so don't even go there.

Oh, but he *was* going there. And the tug of reality that tried to hold him back was softening with each and every step.

Anita's headstone stood before him now; smooth, black, and ominous. Brian reached down and pushed her new bouquet into a planter with the last, their colors clashing like warring rainbows. He then removed his cell phone from its holster, his hands trembling so badly that he didn't think he could dial a number if his life depended on it.

"Is it you?" he whispered to the rock that bore her name and the span of her life as if it were the answer to some trivia question. "Why now? What do you want?"

The phone vibrated in his hands and James Blunt began singing in that high-pitched whine.

This time, Brian was quick to answer. He jerked the phone up to his ear and said, "Hello?"

Static was the only reply.

"Anita?" Tears filled his eyes. He blinked them onto his cheek and wiped them away with the cuff of his jacket. "Anita, is it really you?"

Still nothing but static.

Brian spun, looking at the crop of stone markers that surrounded him, at the forest of trees beyond. Was someone watching him? Trying to push him over the edge? "Who the hell is this?"

The line went dead and the phone vibrated against his ear. He yanked it down to read the screen.

YOU HAVE 1 NEW MESSAGE.

He ran a hand down his face, glossing his stubbled cheeks and jaw with fresh tears, then he touched his screen in habitual sequence, his finger shaking uncontrollably. When he opened the text, terror tore through him as if he'd been stabbed with an icicle.

I WANT YOU, LOVER <3

Brian fell to his knees in the soft grass, staring at those glowing white words on his black screen, then at the etched white words on black stone in front of him. He paused a moment, thumbed his way into his call log, and found "Unknown Caller" listed again and again. He touched one of the entries and hit "call."

The image of a receiver filled his screen, curved lines radiating outward from it as colored dots chased below.

He knelt there in the grass, holding his phone and his breath, listening. At first, the only sound was that of the breeze through leaf-laden branches, but then he heard it. The tone was muffled, but unmistakable. Brian leaned down, pressed his ear against the dirt, unable to believe it.

From below, Anita's cell phone rang.

———

Brian didn't see any other mourners on the grounds that evening, but he thought it best to wait for the cover of darkness, just in case. And so he drove around. The next few hours were a blur. Did he stop somewhere and eat? Yes, he must have.

Finally, just before midnight, he returned to Chapel Hill. The cemetery was in a rural area; there were no wrought iron fences or cathedral gates to keep trespassers out, and so he drove right in. He parked his car, got what he needed from the trunk, and as he moved between the headstones, flashlight in one gloved hand and spade propped up on his shoulder, he was all too aware that he now walked a dangerous tightrope of rationality.

The cell phone had probably shifted. That was all. Something was coming into contact with its touch screen, dialing and relaying old messages to the number Anita had called most often in life: his number. Yes, that was the most reasonable explanation.

But still, he needed to be sure.

He could go through legal channels and have her exhumed. That's exactly what he *should* do. But that would take time. Too much time.

If the calls went on much longer, if he had to read more of those loving texts, had to see that little heart signature again and again, he really would lose his footing, and madness was waiting, all too eager to catch his fall.

Brian tightened his grip on the spade handle. It had rained heavily within the last week. The ground should be soft, the digging easy.

Your back will be the judge of that, my friend.

Yes, it would indeed. Even now, as he climbed the steep hill that gave this place its name, the muscles in his calves and lower back were already blazing. But he could deal with the pain. It was nothing compared to the suffering he'd endured this past year without her. If there was even a chance—

No! She can't still be alive. You know that, don't you? There was an autopsy. She was embalmed! And even if she'd somehow managed to be buried alive, she's been down there for over a year. She would've died of asphyxiation long before now.

Yes, he knew all of that. And yet, all the logic in the world could not stifle his hopes for some kind of reunion.

Oh, if you go ahead with this, you'll see her again all right. Are you ready for that? Ready to see what time and rot have done to that beauty you remember?

Brian didn't allow himself to think about it any further. Instead, he continued up the hill with slow deliberation. He'd been back and forth to this grave so many times over the last year that there should have been a path worn in the grass, but it was just as lush and green as the rest of the grounds.

At last, he found Anita's stone. This was it. He was really going to do this. He lowered the light to the flowers he'd left for her, then to the patch of earth where he was prepared to dig.

Someone beat him to it.

Brian's stomach sank like a stone down a deep well and his legs turned to rubber. He dropped his spade, gripped his flashlight with both hands, trying to steady the quivering beam and train it back on the hole.

It wasn't possible.

The dirt was not piled to one side the way he'd planned to do it. No. The earth was heaped all around the opening, reminding him of the rabbit holes he'd seen in Bugs Bunny cartoons, as if something dug *up* rather than down.

He crept up toward the edge, aimed his flashlight into the hole, and his breath caught in his throat. Anita's coffin was down there, open. The latch had been splintered, the fabric lining stained and torn, but his wife wasn't inside.

Anita was gone.

Brian shined his light around for clues. There were indentations in the dirt around the mouth of the pit—deep grooves made by fingers clawing at the soft earth. He saw shoe prints too, one on top of another; not the tell-tale treads of a sneaker, but rather the smooth indentations of a dress shoe.

He tilted his light up, found clumps of mud flattening the tall grass, moving away from the desecrated grave, moving back down the hill toward the road.

My Anita. Someone's taken her. She's—

Out for a little stroll.

A short burst of laughter escaped Brian's lips, and he pressed a fist against his mouth to muffle the sound. He stood there for a long moment, staring at those muddy clumps, the flashlight wobbling in his hand, and then his cell phone vibrated on his belt.

He flinched, but did not answer it immediately. He knew what the display screen would tell him: he had a new message.

Don't look at it. You see that trail that leads off into darkness? Well, that message is going to tell you where it ends, and you don't want to know. You really don't.

Oh, but he did. He really did.

Brian's hand seemed to move for the phone in slow motion. He opened the text, the message glowing brightly there in the darkness, but he was unprepared for what it said.

COME HOME. I'M WAITING <3

———

The door was open.

How could it be open? Didn't I lock it before I left this morning? Set the alarm?

In his haste to get to the cellular store, he must have forgotten.

Yes. That must've been it.

Brian walked inside in a daze. He shut the door behind him. This time, he made certain it was locked.

There were muddy tracks across his tiled floor; shoe prints, the same smooth sole he'd seen at the cemetery.

He stared at them, his back against the door, swaying on his feet as if he might pass out. For a moment, he had the urge to flee, to run from the house he and Anita had shared, leave it for the last time and never look back. But the impulse was short-lived.

His cell phone vibrated, and like Pavlov's dog, Brian reached for it and read the message off his screen.

COME TO ME, LOVER <3

STRAITJACKET MEMORIES • 173

Yes, dear.

He put the phone away and followed the shoe prints through the foyer and toward the stairs, staggering on his own shaky legs, reaching out for the wall on several occasions to steady himself.

A woman's shoe laid on its side on the first step. Brian picked it up and turned it over in his quivering hands. A black pump; it was muddy, worn, but he recognized it as Anita's just the same.

Three steps up, he completed the pair, and he noticed that those shoe prints had now become foot prints on the carpeted stairs. Small feet, clearly drawn in filth. Brian followed them up.

What was left of Anita's black dress, the dress she'd been buried in, draped the top few steps. It looked like it had been through Hell. Perhaps it had been. Brian remembered the tears he'd shed when he picked it out of her closet and gave it to the mortician, and his eyes blurred all over again.

He felt that impulse to turn and run again, the tug of reason, pulling him back down toward the front door and his car beyond. And this time, it was much stronger than before—he even felt the teeth of his car keys bite his leg through the lining of his pants pocket.

Come on, my friend, don't do this. You've been through a rough patch, but you can still have a full life without her. You can start over in a new city. Maybe Chicago, or New York. A better life! Hey, when life hands you lemons, you make lemonade, right?

"Shut up!" Brian screamed aloud to the empty room, tired of talking to himself, tired of being alone.

He dropped Anita's grimy shoe, wiped his hands on his pants, and slowly climbed into the upstairs hall.

Their bedroom door stood ajar; he lurched toward it, pushed it open.

The stench washed over him like a wave, and Brian withdrew from it, coughing and retching. He gripped the door frame, doubled over, and his stomach gave a violent heave, but nothing spewed from his lips but clear fluid. He loosened his tie, wiped his mouth with the back of his hand, then he pressed his head against the cool wall. Brian stood there wheezing, but after a while—a few seconds or a few minutes, he'd lost all sense of time—he finally gained control of his nausea, rose up and looked into the room.

There was something there. A dark, feminine shape lying naked on the bed they'd shared, waiting for him.

"Anita?" Brian whispered. "Oh my God, is it really you?"

A small light came on, illuminating long, bony fingers; it took him a moment to realize it was the screen of her cell phone.

His own phone vibrated, and this time he was quick to answer it.

LEAVE THE LIGHTS OFF <3

Brian nodded.
Yes, my love, we wouldn't want to spoil the illu—
We wouldn't want to spoil the mood.
He unbuttoned his shirt, and went to her.

Reason made one final plea, dragging out all the old banalities. *You can't live in the past.*

Yes, Brian knew that. There was no going back now. This would be a fresh start for both of them; a second wedding night.

Life goes on.

Yes it does. Brian left his pants on the floor and crawled into bed. *And when life hands you lemons, you make lemonade. Isn't that right?*

Anita's perfume was no longer sweet, and when he ran his fingers through her hair, it came out of her moldering scalp in dry clumps. His arms went around her gaunt waist, pulled her to him. Her skin was cold—her emaciated breasts like two glaciers pressed against his chest—but when he felt her lower body against his groin, he stiffened just the same.

Brian kissed her. Her lips were dry, thin, wrinkled and leathery, and he could feel the hardness of her teeth beneath. And when he looked deep into her eyes, he saw dark sockets that mirrored nothing. But it was *her.* It was really her. Somehow, his wife was back in his arms again, and he knew it was no fantasy this time.

He was no longer alone, and he would never be without her again.

NOTES

There you are, faithful readers! You made it through the darkness, through all the weird twists and turns, and with your sanity more or less intact. Well done! See, I told you that you'd be fine if you just followed the path.

Now, however, I'm afraid we've come to that sign post up ahead. You know...the one with a little warning. You've seen them before, haven't you? Big, bold letters on a tree, or a fence, or a map that say things like BEWARE OF DOG, or maybe HERE THERE BE TIGERS! Well, faithful readers, your sign reads HERE THERE BE SPOILERS!

If you've read *Skull Full of Kisses*, you're familiar with what I do here. This is where I give you the stories *behind* the stories featured in this collection. And in some cases, I just might let a few details slip, details that may just ruin the endings for you. So, if you've followed that dark and winding path all the way up to this point, please, by all means, continue on. If not, if you tried to take a shortcut after only a tale or two, well... enter at your own risk!

———

Don't Let the Bed Bugs Bite

If you've read much of my work, you might have noticed a re-occurring theme: anything with more than four legs is evil. I have been a life-long arachnophobe, so spiders have been a frequent guest in my nightmares over the years, but centipedes, ants...any bug will give me chills and make my skin crawl. So, travelling as much as I do, and staying in many different hotels for conventions and book signings, it was only natural that I become totally paranoid about bed bugs.

In fact, I was packing for a convention in Columbus, Ohio, when I made the mistake of reading an article on the little blood-suckers. Turns out, there had been a huge infestation in— you guessed it— Columbus, Ohio. I immediately freaked out and started sealing all my clothes in plastic Zip-lock bags. I wanted to take every precaution to make sure that, if there *were* any bugs where I was going, I didn't bring any home with me.

All of this got me thinking...What if these little vampires were just that: little vampires? I did some research into various vampire myths and legends from around the world, and I came across the African *Adze*: a creature of the night that turns into an insect! After that, the story came together very quickly.

One of my favorite moments—when the *Adze* actually turns into a mass of crawling, squirming bugs—was suggested to me by friend and writer Sara Larson. She read an early draft of the story and said she wanted to see something like the scene in *Bram Stoker's Dracula*, but with the vampire becoming a pile of bugs instead of rats. It was a great idea (Sara always had such great ideas), and I'm so glad I took her advice.

————

Flowers in Winter

Bram Stoker Award-winning editor Michael Knost did a series of anthologies called *Legends of the Mountain State*, focused on the various myths and legends of West Virginia. Michael asked me to submit a story to the third volume of the series, and the legend he gave me—the Romeo and Juliet-style story of the old North house in Lewisburg—seemed tailor made for me.

I've said it before and I'll say it again: everything I write is a love story—a dark, twisted love story. My tales all seem to deal with some form of relationship. Instead of normal, everyday life complications, however, my characters' problems are of the supernatural variety.

————

The Grove

A few years ago, I was asked to submit a tale to an anthology called *Up Jumped the Devil*, a book of stories inspired by the songs of Nick Cave and the Bad Seeds. The concept was for each author to take a song and write a tale from it. Not a literal translation, mind you, but every author's own interpretation.

I was given a choice of several songs to draw from, but the floral imagery in "Bring It On" really spoke to me. I'd wanted to do a story about people turning into plants for years now, and this seemed like the perfect excuse to finally make that happen.

The anthology was never published, however, so I had to shop the orphaned tale around. One editor dubbed it "that tree-fucking story," which still tickles me to this day. For a time, it was slated to be published in *Shroud Magazine* #13, but the last issue *Shroud* published before going on permanent hiatus was #12, so the tale was orphaned for a second time.

It appears here for the first time anywhere.

———

Sandwalkers

This tale began with me doing research on various myths from around the world. I'd been asked to submit something for an anthology of monster tales called *Fell Beasts*, and I wanted to do something that really hadn't been done before— something other than the usual suspects of werewolves, vampires, and zombies. When I read about the Persian legend of the Manticore —a creature that was part lion, part scorpion, and part bat, I thought it would make the perfect villain for a horror story.

I've also wanted to do a military tale for a while now, and given the area where the Manticore stories originated, I felt this would be a perfect opportunity. I probably did more research on that aspect of the tale than on the monsters, making sure everything rang true and felt authentic. To ensure this, I showed the finished manuscript to an ex-marine. He gave me one piece of advice. At one point, I had Miller take his weapon apart, clean it, then put it back together. I wanted to show the corporal's skill and commitment, but my friend said, "No marine would field strip a rifle under those circumstances."

————

In Vino Veritas

Of all the stories in this collection, this was probably the most fun to do. Written for the Urban Fantasy Noir anthology *Streets of Shadows*, this was the first time I had ever collaborated with another author. And what a pleasure it was to work with a writer like Tim Waggoner!

Tim is the author of fantasy and horror novels for both adults and young readers. His works including the *Nekropolis* and *Night Terrors* series, and he also teaches creative writing—at both Sinclair Community College and in Seton Hill University's MFA in Writing Popular Fiction program.

The way we worked is that I would write a section of the story, and then I would hand it off to Tim. Tim would then up the ante and leave me with a cliffhanger. My mouth would drop, I'd say, "Shit, I didn't see that coming," and then I'd be forced to go on from there and try to raise the stakes even more.

It was a wonderful experience, one I hope to have again in the future.

Due to space concerns with the *Streets of Shadows* anthology, "*In Vino Veritas*" was heavily edited for its initial printing. While I felt many of those cuts made it a better tale, there was material from inside the speakeasy that I hated to see go. Those excised passages have been restored here, making this the first time the story has appeared in its original form.

———

For the River is Wide and the Gods are Hungry

"For the River is Wide and the Gods are Hungry" was first written for an anthology on Appalachian wives' tales. I wanted to do something cool, like why people cover mirrors after someone dies, but no, all of those myths were already taken. Instead, the editor asked me to do a story based on the old wives' tale: "You never swim across the river during the Dog Days of Summer."

Despite my initial lack of enthusiasm, I think I was able to pull off a pretty good horror story. The anthology, however, fell apart and was never published. Still, the story was put out as a stand-alone tale in various eBook formats.

This is the first time it has appeared in print.

The long title is a tribute to the great Harlan Ellison, who wrote an episode of *Star Trek* called "For All the World Is Hollow and I Have Touched the Sky." Possibly the longest title in history!

———

Masako's Tale

Originally titled "Blood and Silk," this story was written for the second *Beast Within* anthology of shape-shifter tales. I wanted to tell a Beauty and the Beast-style story from the point of view of the beast. I also love Asian culture and mythology, and the legend of the *Jorōgumo* seemed like a great basis for a horror story.

The ending of this story was quite a bit longer in its initial draft. I had Masako take her instrument, her *biwa*, out onto the front step of her shack and play a tune, trying to drown out the sounds of her children feeding on her only love. My pre-readers, however, suggested that I cut it off where it ends now, leaving what happens next to the readers' imaginations. I hated making that edit at first, but I think they were right.

————

Hell's Hollow

I'd never written a zombie story before. One day, I was sitting around and the idea hit me: a zombie remake of *High Noon*, but the duel just keeps on happening again and again, because, well, the sheriff and the outlaw are zombies. I kicked the idea around in my head for a while, trying to think of a way to make it work. Then, I got another burst of inspiration: what if the zombies don't know they're dead?

One day, a call went out for tales for a Weird Western anthology, and I sat down and wrote "Hell's Hollow." The western anthology fell through a few months later, but I really liked the story a lot. I sat down, changed the setting from a desert ghost town to a forgotten village in the mountains, and sold the revised tale to APEX for their *Appalachian Undead* anthology.

Actually, I sold the story to them twice. The first time, they wanted it, but then one of the editors asked me to change the sheriff and the outlaw to the Hatfields and McCoys. I really didn't want to do that, so I withdrew from the project. The editors really loved the story, however, so later they came back to me and asked for the story again without any changes.

Inner Goddess

Author Maurice Broaddus told me about an upcoming anthology called *The Book of the Dead* from an English publisher, Jurassic London. It was to be a collection of mummy stories to benefit the Egyptian Society of London, and the special edition hardcover of the book would actually be mummified! Something that cool, I could not pass up!

Egyptian gods have always fascinated me, and as I busied myself with research into mummification, I came across images of cats that had been turned into mummies by priests who worshipped Bast. They were so incredibly creepy! I knew instantly that I had to write about them.

As for the human angle, I knew I wanted to tell a tale of a submissive girl who finds her inner strength and turns the table on her abuser. I went to my bondage expert (Yes, I have an expert for just about everything), and I asked her about handcuffs and how they would feel, if they left marks, etc. She asked me what the story was about and I told her, "Mummies." Her response: "Egyptian, or BDSM?" My jaw literally dropped.

The rest, as they say, is history.

Unknown Caller

Written for the *Cadence in Decay* anthology, which was to have come from another UK publisher, Mansion House Books. All the stories had to deal with some form of communication. I remember thinking about the old *Twilight Zone* episode, "Night Call," about an elderly woman who gets a phone call from beyond the grave, and I wanted to update it a bit using text messages.

I wondered if anyone had ever been buried with their cell phone?

In doing research, I found out that, not only had a woman been buried with her cell phone in England, but her family now believed she was texting them from her coffin! As the news story went, the husband and children were getting messages from her number, messages that she used to send to them when she was alive. And so, my mind took that to the next step and asked, "What if they went and dug her back up?"

It was a difficult story to write.

My friend, author Sara Larson, had just died of cancer, and as I was still grieving for her, my wife was diagnosed with a different form of the disease as well. I began to wonder just how far grief could drive a man, and, as you can see, my mind went to a very dark place.

One morning, my son came downstairs while I was making coffee and he read what was on my laptop screen. It was the end of the story. He looked over at me, shook his head, and asked, "How do you sleep at night?"

Thankfully, my wife was able to be treated surgically, and as I write this, she has made a successful recovery and is cancer free. *Cadence in Decay*, however, could not rebound from various contractual and financial obstacles. The anthology fell apart, and "Unknown Caller" appears here in print for the first time.

———

Well, faithful readers, it looks like we've once again reached the end of the road. That old, creaky door is about to swing shut again, sealing all those unfathomable shadows inside. But they won't stay locked away forever. There are always more tales waiting to be told.

As always, I've enjoyed our time together, and I look forward to seeing you again very soon. Perhaps, when you least expect it.

So, until next time, I will quote the original Horror Host, *The Inner Sanctum's* Raymond Edward Johnson: "Pleasant dreeeeaaams, hmmmmm?"

ACKNOWLEDGMENTS

I want to thank my family, especially my wife, Stephanie, and my sons, Kyle and Ryan, for their never-ending love and support; Tony Acree and the entire staff at Hydra Publications; Natasha Altericii for her amazing cover art; actress, singer, model, Kelly Abbass, one of my oldest and dearest on-line friends, for the inspiration and the support; authors and editors Maurice Broaddus, Jennifer Brozek, Jerry Gordon, Jackie Gamber, Michael Knost, Ty Schwamberger, Jared Shurin, Jason Sizemore, and Tim Waggoner; all the Indiana Horror Writers; and, of course, my faithful readers everywhere.

ABOUT THE AUTHOR

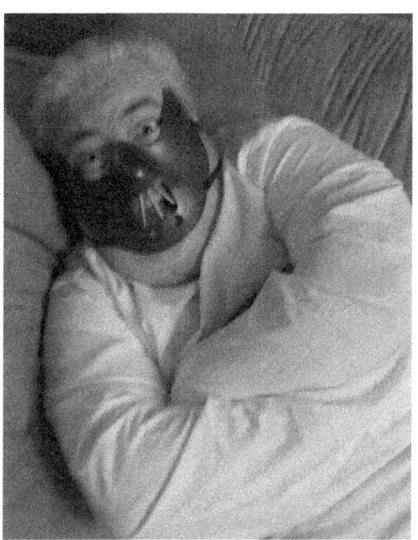

Michael West is the bestselling author of *Cinema of Shadows,
Spook House, The Wide Game, Skull Full of Kisses*, and the criti-
cally- acclaimed *Legacy of the Gods* series. He lives and works
in the Indianapolis area with his wife, their two children, and
their dog, King Seesar.

Writing keeps him sane.